BROKEN MAGE

BROKEN PEAK PACK
BOOK 3

BY JULES CRISARE

BROKEN PEAK PACK

Broken Hero
Broken Sage
Broken Mage
Broken Rebel
Broken Crown
Broken Witch

HIDDEN RUNAWAYS

Hidden Trouble

BLACK HILLS VENDETTA

Wolf's Retribution
Wolf's Revenge
Wolf's Reckoning (*coming to Kickstarter in 2024*)

BOX SETS

Broken Peak Pack eBook Bundle Volume 1
Broken Peak Pack eBook Bundle Volume 2
Broken Peak Pack Omnibus Collector's Edition (*Kickstarter Exclusive*)

SILVER SENTINEL NOVELS

Destined Heir
The Last Immortal Mystery Files (*coming to Kickstarter in 2023*)

SENTINELS OF THE SILVER ORB

BROKEN MAGE

BROKEN PEAK PACK
BOOK 3

BY JULES CRISARE

SILVER ORB BOOKS

BROKEN MAGE

Designed by J. Crisare

0123pbk

ISBN: 978-1-948603-29-4 (pbk.)

*For small-batch bourbon.
You get me through so many phases of
publishing a book. Although, you tend to
hinder more than help the actual writing.
For that reason (and for hindering two
chapters, which were brilliant when I wrote
them, but a hot mess the next morning), this
is only a 90% dedication.
The remaining 10% of the dedication goes
to the industrial-sized bottle of Advil that
gets me through the mornings after the small-
batch bourbon nights.*

PROLOGUE

A History of Shifters & the Role of the McCallisters
—from Edna McCallister's journal

IN THE beginning, when the Great Shifters ruled from the skies, the wizards, witches, and vampires hadn't yet formed an alliance to wage a massive war against the Great Shifters. A wizard with barely enough power to be called a wizard lived in the outskirts of supernatural society. Ostracized by the other wizards and ignored by the vampires and witches.

The wizard searched for ways to gain more power. Eventually, they stood before the leaders of the Great Shifters begging for help.

Normally, the Great Shifters didn't involve themselves in the affairs of the supernaturals, but they knew the war was approaching and had been carefully setting the pieces in place for the future when shifters and supernaturals would need to unite under the Hero.

But the Hero would need help from others in order to succeed, and a wizard who didn't understand the strength of their power, made the wizard a perfect pawn in the Great Shifters' plan.

The power wielded by wizards had always been overt and flashy by most standards. This outcast differed from the others. The wizard's power was a subtle influence that shared the world around them.

The Great Shifters offered the wizard and the wizard's descendants protection, knowing the time would come when the Hero would need someone capable of manipulating minor details and events that would ensure success. When the time was right, the Mage would be born and stand by the Hero's side, ensuring success.

CHAPTER ONE

LEIGHTON wandered through the silent lodge. Everyone was asleep. Well, practically everybody. It was Jackson's night to patrol. Ever since Broken Peak faced two attacks by forces intent on taking Jackson's son away, they safeguarded the territory borders during the night. The pack didn't have adequate numbers to sustain the rigorous schedule, but the other shifters in the area volunteered to help.

Roose, the resident curmudgeon and bear shifter, plus Gareth and the other mountain lions reinforced the pack's skeleton crew. Even Mac, the old coyote shifter, put a few hours in the woods every night. For the time being, the pack managed, but Leighton knew they couldn't keep it up for long. The combination of routine and exhaustion would lead to someone overlooking the signs of a raid.

And next time, the pack wouldn't be so lucky.

Vixen, his Alpha female, was a formidable ally with a deadly griffin lurking inside her, but she couldn't hold the government off indefinitely. And once the government figured out what animal hid beneath her skin, they'd redouble their efforts. The military, or whatever agency was intent on seizing the four-year-old boy, had limitless funds, better weapons, and an infinite supply of warm bodies to hurl at the pack. Eventually the government would prevail. Broken Peak only had a Vixen and a folklorist desperately working to figure out if the volumes filled with the ramblings of long-dead shifters held any true significance or were just gibberish.

Leighton had money on the writers being gibbering idiots.

On the nights when Leighton wasn't slated for patrol, he'd wake up throughout the night and couldn't get back to sleep until he confirmed everyone was secure and asleep in their beds. He started with the Alphas, never actually opening the door to check and instead relying on noises to confirm all was well. Usually, it was Bray snoring, but occasionally it was just the sound of a blanket shifting against a sheet. Then he moved on to his packmates, starting with the youngest, Tevin, and moving up to the oldest, Jackson. He checked on Foster last. Foster might have been Jackson and Eleanor's son, but he was the pack's pup too.

The only room he entered belonged to Foster. Both Leighton and his wolf didn't rely on sleeping noises, they required the comfort of contact.

Leighton pushed wide the door. Expecting the same quiet silence he encountered every other night, he was unprepared for the pressure of the heated air that twisted across the floor and nearly flattened him.

Smoke.

Heavy smoke.

Warmth. No. Not warmth.

Heat.

Burning heat.

Fire. The room was on fire.

Leighton stepped into the room, but with each step the bed moved further away.

The smoke grew heavier and despite his best efforts to draw oxygen into his lungs; he failed. Falling to the floor, he dragged his body toward the bed. For every inch he gained, the bed pulled back a foot.

Panic won its battle, and Leighton's heart pounded against his ribs. His lungs ached and his palms burned, but he refused to admit defeat. Leighton raised his head, searching for the bed, for Foster's tiny body under the blankets, but the bed was gone.

The room disappeared.

Leighton stood in the middle of the forest, glowing orange as the flames danced and hopped from tree to tree.

Foster shifted back and forth from boy to wolf, less than fifty feet away from Leighton.

The fire crept closer, but ignored Leighton. It wasn't hungry for the male. The fire wanted the boy. Leighton let out a roar, dug his feet into the ground and raced for the boy. He could beat the flames if he just moved fast enough. He covered half the distance, but Foster had moved no closer.

Foster's cries grew louder than the howling of the flames, but Leighton still couldn't reach him. Leighton drew strength from some unknown reserve deep within him and shoved hard off his feet. Except instead of driving forward, his feet sank into the soft ground. Leighton struggled to wrench his legs free, but the earth swallowed his ankles, locking him in place.

The land, his land, betrayed him and aligned itself with the fire. The earth would absorb Foster's ashes. It would take its payment. Leighton was powerless to do anything except watch. He would be witness to a pup's death. He'd have to be the one to return home and confess his failure. Leighton couldn't save Foster.

Leighton wasn't worthy.

As the fire licked at Foster's skin, and the boy's cries of fear changed to wails of pain, Leighton screamed with him.

The roar of the fire eased and the cries of the pup faded, but Leighton's scream pierced the night.

"Leighton?" Vixen knelt in front of him.

His mouth snapped shut, and he jerked his head back, striking the hard surface of the wall. Several blinks later and he found himself in the corner of his room, squeezed between the dresser and his bed. "A dream?"

Vixen nodded and reached her hand toward him. The next step in their dance required him to take her hand. She never touched him first. They'd performed this maneuver enough times. He recognized the cues. Even Bray, lurking in the hallway just outside the door and observing his mate, knew what transpired next.

Vixen had a limitless reservoir of patience. Kneeling in front of him with an outstretched palm, she would wait all night if she had to until he placed his hand in hers. Leighton had no problem sitting on the floor all night, but he wouldn't inflict his penance on his Alphas.

He wrapped his hand around hers and they helped each other to their feet.

"Let's get you into bed. I've slept on enough floors to know a bed is preferable." She brought him to his bed and straightened the sheets and blankets he tore off the mattress during his nightmare.

Once the bed had been restored and Leighton was back under the covers, Vixen sat down next to him. He'd gotten better over the months. He no longer clung to her until sleep returned. Leighton closed his eyes and counted to thirty. Most nights, Vixen left him alone before he reached twenty. Tonight was not most nights.

"They're getting worse. You need to talk about them. It doesn't have to be me, but you need to tell someone or the nightmares will consume you."

He said nothing. Seconds afterward, Vixen squeezed his shoulder and left him alone in his bedroom.

Leighton wasn't worthy.

He wasn't worthy of the pack, he wasn't worthy of Vixen's attention, and he wasn't worthy of a mate.

CHAPTER TWO

DANIELLE Howe stepped out of the coffee shop with a large quad vanilla breve latte in each hand and zigzagged around the press of morning commuters, making their progress to the Metro or the bus stand. She envied them their relaxed commute. They spent the morning reading the latest news off their phone or chuckling at the newest meme making its way through any of the social media sites. While Danielle spent an hour every morning traveling less than fifteen miles, driving along what had to be the most congested freeways in the country. Unfortunately, the only means to commute to her job without a car required riding two trains, one bus, and walking the final bit because protocol prevented anyone not welcome from making it past the security gate.

Holding the coffee in front of her, she maneuvered her way through the throng until she was no longer moving against the tide of bodies and found a clear route to her white 1961 P1800 without worry of spilling her coffee. She set her drinks on the car roof, then unlocked and opened the front door. Without a cup holder and unable to find one that fit the interior of her old car, she stabilized the two cups of coffee between her thighs. Danielle's current record for the number of coffees transported without incident sat at three. She wasn't brave enough to tackle four.

Danielle started her car and pulled out into traffic. On a good day, she spent most of the time in third gear while driving in the city. Most days she remained in second gear with the occasional tease of third. Her knees hated her and mutinied against her usage of a manual transmission with spasms and pangs found on retired athletes twice her age. But none of that mattered. Danielle would accept the need for knee-replacement surgery before she was thirty as compensation for driving one of the coolest cars ever driven by a secret agent. She might not be a spy, but she drove the same car as one. Well, that and she inherited it from her grammy, and truly, the prospect of purchasing a new vehicle, even a new-to-her vehicle, terrorized the hell out of her.

Any large payment, even a car payment, would set off alarms and she'd go through a round of questioning that consisted of multiple polygraphs and several interrogations. Five months ago, she wouldn't have minded. But five months ago she hadn't broken Company rules and committed treason among several other crimes. Not that it mattered, since they could take her off the sidewalk and bring her to the Mansion for questioning without a warrant. And treason wasn't the transgression that had her looking over her shoulder while struggling to act as normal as possible. Betraying Unit D was her actual crime. Although, in her defense, Unit D betrayed one of their own first and earned whatever misery she dished out to them from behind her computer.

The traffic light turned yellow before she turned right onto Third. Sure, she could have risked it, but Danielle had a theory that in an alternate reality, this intersection was a portal to hell and some evilness seeped through. It was the only explanation for the terror the intersection was capable of producing in drivers, bicyclists, and pedestrians alike. Her foot punched against the clutch and she popped the shifter into neutral, waiting for the traffic light to change from red to green. Her little car didn't stand a chance against the heavy traffic barreling down Third from Massachusetts.

The passenger door opened and an older man dropped into the seat, closing the door and securing the lap belt before Danielle registered his presence.

"Holy Crap!"

The man reached across the car's interior and captured one of the coffees from her lap. "Thanks."

"Jeesh. You can't do that. You can't just jump into my car like that. First, it's scary, and second, it's creepy, General Jesup."

"The light changed, Ms. Howe. Unless you prefer to attract attention to yourself, I recommend turning on to Third as planned." The General sipped the coffee and clicked his tongue behind his teeth at the sweetness of the drink. "Get on 395. We'll be taking 81 South."

"Um? We are?" Danielle asked and wondered how she evolved into a "we" and where the freshly minted "we" was headed.

General Jesup looked over his shoulder and out the back window, "take the next left. Don't signal, just yank the wheel hard left."

"But-"

"No buts. Just do it." For the next twenty minutes, Danielle almost caused at least five car accidents and was definitely the cause of one fender bender as General Jesup navigated her along a roundabout route to 395. "Okay, take this exit and merge into the center lane, follow traffic until 81 south, but be prepared to get off the highway at my say so."

Danielle's knee protested the detour. She probably should have protested her carjacking as well, but the General hadn't steered her wrong yet. She delivered intelligence to him, and he gave that intelligence to the former Unit D member code named Vixen. During the last several months, they kept Vixen informed and alive. And now the General appeared to be doing the same for Danielle.

She picked up her neglected and partially cooled coffee, which hadn't splashed a single drop during her impromptu evasive driving lesson, and guzzled half the cup's contents. She set the drink back between her thighs and gripped the steering wheel. Between the incessant shifting before they got on the highway and the General's less than stellar detour, Danielle's hand hadn't lifted off the gear shifter. For the first time since receiving the classic car, she secretly wished she had an automatic transmission. So did her knee.

"So, um, are you planning on sharing the reason for what every rational human being would recognize as a carjacking?"

The General closed his eyes and pushed his head against the small headrest. "You couldn't be one of those persons who bought a nice SUV with heated seats that reclined?"

"You're dodging my question."

"Ms. Howe, you're an exceptionally intelligent woman. If you weren't, you wouldn't hold the job you have."

"Not certain I still have that job."

"Be that as it may, the Company wouldn't have recruited and enticed you into the fold then assigned to the Unit if you weren't the smartest person in the room. I'm confident you can put the pieces together and come up with a logical explanation for this morning's events without me spelling it out for you."

Danielle glanced over and narrowed her eyes at him before returning her attention to the roadway in front of her. "Is this a test?"

"No, but I haven't slept in twenty-six hours and spending another
hour explaining the minutia is robbing me of an opportunity to find a
little sleep before I endure another twenty-four hours of not sleeping."
General Jesup shifted his weight until he located a modest amount of
comfort, suitable for a nap.

Twenty-six hours! What happened in the previous twenty-four
hours that led to a man not sleeping and how come she was involved?
Well, no, that wasn't accurate. She knew precisely why she was involved.
The General wasn't mistaken in his appraisal of her intelligence. Except
the Company never recruited her. They offered a choice: work for them
or go to prison. Danielle opted for the former, as the latter would be
worse than anything she imagined.

The Company disappeared her, which wasn't difficult considering
she was an only child who spoke with her parents maybe once a month.
She likewise wasn't the type of person who accumulated close friends
during her childhood, or even her adulthood. She'd never met her closest friends since they only communicated in the secluded recesses
of the internet, far away from the curious lurkers or technologically
unskilled. The men from the Company didn't look at it that way, and
chances were whatever judge they found wouldn't see it that way either,
hence accepting their job offer.

In the long run she was well compensated to burrow into the secrets
of the men and women Unit D targeted. Danielle might have been doing
not good things, but she was doing it to not good people who would, in
turn, do not good things to good people if she didn't stop them.

Danielle was like Vixen in that way. Both women did bad things to
bad people, so good people remained safe. Or relatively safe. So when
the order arrived for some of Unit D's newer recruits to retire Vixen,

Danielle did what she felt was right and composed a mission packet loaded with somewhat modified data. Enough clues for someone as vigilant as Vixen to pick up, but could be explained away as mistakes if ever noticed.

Danielle didn't believe Vixen's failed retirement was the reason for General Jesup carjacking her, so it had to be something else. Not the second attempt to remove Vixen either. Officially, Danielle didn't know anything about that failed mission. The General told her about it when she discovered Unit D had the little boy, Foster, in their sights and she contacted the General.

Vixen came into the city for a visit after she learned Foster became a target. Not that anyone talked about the visit. No, they whispered about the presents she left for the men who ran the Company and the man who was their boss.

That left Foster and Vixen's subsequent visit as the likely reason Danielle and General Jesup were heading south.

To 81.

To Broken Peak.

Oh crap!

Danielle was headed to Broken Peak Pack. That had to be where General Jesup wanted to go. Danielle hadn't formally met Vixen, but couldn't wait for the chance to finally see the legend of Unit D in person.

"I don't think we're being followed, but they presumably don't believe they have to. They know where we're headed."

"Hm?" General Jesup didn't open his eyes.

"If they realize you're with me, then they know the only place we'd be headed and don't have to follow us."

"Took you longer than I expected."

"My mind drifted for a moment before circling back on track. Are they aware we're coming?"

Danielle fantasized about meeting Vixen and the others who lived with her, but not like this. A surprise appearance in Broken Peak's Pack territory might not result in ice cream and cake. Not that shifters—during a conversation with the General, he cautioned Danielle that Vixen had advised him the term werewolf was pejorative—would have greeted her with ice cream and cake. Beer and barbecue were more likely.

"We have to assume the sat phone is compromised."

"No shit. I warned you the right person could break into the signal in seconds and listen in on the call in real time."

"Ms. Howe, someone would have to first break the cipher, of which there are a minimal number of individuals capable of performing such a task. Then they'd have to realize the call was being made and intercept it, of which there are much fewer individuals with such knowledge. Besides, it's an excellent way to deliver misleading information until we can find out who is listening in." General Jesup smirked, but his eyes remained closed. "Now, if you don't mind, I'm napping."

"It's a six-hour trip."

"Perfect. I'll catch up on my sleep."

Before Danielle asked further questions, a quiet snore escaped from the General's open mouth.

What did you know? He could sleep anywhere.

Danielle flipped between NPR and classic rock stations on her radio. She never contemplated why she was traveling south at the insistence of an elderly man or what it meant for her and her relationship with the Company. She had a decent notion of why and no interest in examining the reasons too closely. Instead, she focused on who she would be visiting.

Danielle knew them all by name. The Company was so concerned about controlling information and stopping it from leaving the building that they weren't nearly as worried about information moving *inside* the building. Between Danielle's clearance and Unit D's role, she could look anywhere without setting off alarms. So, she might have also delved into the pack members' histories and discovered as many pictures as possible. The most recent one had all the men wearing costumes, most of which exposed their chests and left no question whether they were big everywhere. Well, she assumed they were wearing costumes. If the naked chests, tight pants, and loin cloth was how they dressed on a daily basis, Danielle had some major concerns.

Five hours into her drive, she needed to stop for gas. As she slowed down and took the first exit with a sign displaying a gas pump, the General woke up.

General Jesup opened his eyes and glanced out the window while doing his best to stretch in the rather compact P1800. "We haven't been on the road long enough to be there yet."

"My gas tank is almost empty." She pulled up to the pump and while shifting the car into neutral, popping the emergency brake, and turning off the ignition, she dug in her purse for her credit card.

A fifty-dollar bill waved in front of her eyes, "they might expect us to head to the Pack, but we don't need to confirm it."

Danielle snatched the cash from his grip, "Vixen uses her cards."

"Her identities are hidden from the Company. Using her cards doesn't raise flags."

Danielle mumbled something about crazy old men as she exited the car and stomped her way across the parking lot to pay before filling the gas tank. Although paying with a fifty-dollar bill might be more conspicuous than using her charge card.

"Pay after you pump, Ms. Howe."

The General's mocking laughter followed her as she u-turned and headed back to the pump. What should have taken five minutes, ended up taking over fifteen by the time she got the pump running, washed the windshields and headlights, snatched a diet Coke from the cooler, and paid for it all at the counter.

She got back behind the wheel of her P1800 with a huff and handed the General the change. He eyed the cool bottle of soda, then peered at the cash in his palm. "Ms. Howe?"

"Yeah, yeah, fine. What do you want?" She plucked a five-dollar bill from his hand and got back out of her car.

"Schweppes bitter lemon."

There was no way the gas station had bitter lemon. The old man was getting a Sprite and would just have to like it.

CHAPTER THREE

"**YOU** could have mentioned there'd be hiking." Danielle never considered herself athletic and walking from her parking spot at the Company to her office got checked off for exercise in her book. Hiking through the woods along a non-existent trail fell at the bottom of the list of compelling ways to increase her resting heart rate.

"There's a back road, but with Vixen around, it's probably trapped." The General didn't bother looking back when he spoke.

"Yeah, but I'm wearing a skirt," Dani teetered on her definitely *not appropriate for hiking through a forest* shoes and caught a branch so she wouldn't totter. "And high heels, General. I am wearing shoes with heels that make walking on solid ground a challenge. Dirt and roots and leaves and, oh my God, is that a dead toad?"

General Jesup stopped and drew in a deep breath through his nose. "I told you to stay in the car, that I would send someone up to get you."

"And leave me alone for someone from Unit D to find me? No thanks!" Danielle tip-toed around the dead toad. "So, what are they like? You've met them, right?"

"Ms. Howe."

"Well? Are they like the shifters in books? All muscle-bound and Alpha? Oh, do they sparkle?"

"Ms. Howe." General Jesup's annoyance rose.

"Do they hate humans? Is this like a survival camp or something? Jackson's record had some altercations with humans. Is he going to hate us?" Danielle filled in the silence with chatter. She didn't care about the answers, she just couldn't stand not having noise. And since her phone (and credit cards) disappeared from her bag, she assumed the General took them. It made sense that he'd then help her fill-in the silence.

"Jackson has a human mate, remember? You researched Eleanor Ward's background for Vixen. If Jackson hated humans, why would he take a human mate?"

"Maybe he despises her and the mating piece is something he can't control. Like his wolf takes over or something?"

"Why don't you keep a list of all your questions and ask them when we arrive."

"Helllooo, I want them to like me. I have a strong suspicion I am being unloaded and I don't want them hating me."

General Jesup came to a sudden stop and turned to face her. "Why do you suspect you are the one being unloaded and not me or both of us?"

"Because," Danielle yanked her computer bag strap higher on her shoulder, pushed her glasses up her nose, and crossed her arms over her chest. "You wouldn't have used me as a chauffeur, you'd have found a way down here without my help."

"And leave you alone at the Company?" The General turned around and stalked down the barely there trail. "Even if I was the kind of male to leave behind someone to fend for themselves, which I'm not, Vixen would have me drawn and quartered. Hell, she'd probably disembowel me then rip out my spine herself."

Danielle almost toppled over. In her mind, she blamed it on her heels, but in truth, it was the General's offhand remark about Vixen tearing him apart. "She would?"

"Yes, she would. You're hers as much as everyone else she's plucked out of a shit situation." The general hesitated, planted his fists on his hips, and studied the sky. "And right now, you're in the shittiest of shit situations."

"Are you expecting to use celestial navigation to get to wherever it is I'm being dumped? Because the sun's still out and I don't think you can see the stars."

"I'm wondering if it's worth racing to the meeting place and listening to you gripe about the pace, or slow down and spend more time hearing you complain about everything else."

"Hey, I think complaining is an improvement from curling up on the ground and sobbing." Danielle stamped her foot and her heel sank into the earth. She wiggled her heel back and forth until it broke loose. "And if you hadn't taken my phone, a podcast would be entertaining me right now."

"I saw your playlist and, honestly, I am worried our hosts won't enjoy your listening habits."

"Well, it's not like there's an abundance of information available that isn't steeped in the paranormal."

The General continued staring at the sky, refusing to glance at Danielle. "Ms. Howe, listening to amateurs discuss Skinwalker Ranch and the possibility of skinwalkers existing, is not anywhere remotely close to research."

"You don't know that." Danielle walked forward. She bumped against his shoulder as she passed the General, but remained mindful of the battle the ground waged with her shoes. "Maybe they aren't shifters. Maybe they're aliens and strip off their human skin, or maybe they are wolf aliens who strip off their human skin. Or, what if they're like big foots?"

"Big foots?" The General followed her.

"Yeah? What if they're like the wolfman, a sort of bipedal furry creature, and have communities hidden away? And the only reason we never learned about them before Vixen stumbled across them was because they captured anyone who saw them?"

"And how do you know we were unaware of their presence?"

"Oh please," Danielle lifted her arms and flapped her hands at the absurd question and twisted around to confront General Jesup. "If the government knew, I'd have turned up the files. They can't hide them from me. I know what's really in Fort Knox."

"Ms. Howe..."

"And shifters are dangerous. And not just because they're unknown. If Vixen proved anything, it's that normal missions will likely fail. Well, as normal as an assassination mission with a helicopter and a team prepared to eliminate high-risk targets can be deemed normal. No one knows anything about them except that they can take down teams supplied with the latest tech, and they can do it with comparatively primitive equipment. You can't fault me for seeking hints outside the Company. Sure, the podcasts might be ninety-nine percent made up, but I've found leads from a lot less."

A man coughed behind her and Danielle screamed and jumped. Between the massive computer bag and her heels sinking into the earth, she weebled and wobbled. That she didn't fall down was a wonder. Or the benefit of enjoying a lower center of gravity owing to most of her body's mass residing in her hips, butt, and thighs. She gave up on the squats that were supposed to keep her lower body in shape after she wasn't required to attend gym class in school anymore, besides the squats never helped and she enjoyed her breves too much.

"They're right behind me, aren't they?"

The general smiled, "I tried to warn you."

"No, you didn't. You said my last name in the same manner you've said it since you jumped in my car this morning, except this time you included a slight inflection at the end."

He released a long-suffering sigh and Danielle narrowed her eyes at him. If anyone should be sighing, she should be.

"Would you like to meet our hosts? Or would you prefer to keep your back to them and continue our conversation?"

"Neither." Danielle closed her eyes and wished she was anywhere but there. She didn't believe any of what she expressed about shifters being dangerous, but having nothing to base an analysis on, she pulled from the paranormal communities. The one point they all seemed to settle on was that skinwalkers were dangerous. Since the skinwalkers were the closest thing she found to shifters, she relied on the paranormal community for information, even if she didn't trust it.

Kernels of truth were located everywhere.

"I don't believe neither is an option, Ms. Howe."

"Well, until you add having the ground swallowing me whole, I'm sticking with neither."

A deep laugh rumbled from behind her, sending shivers along Danielle's spine.

"Looks like the ground is already doing a decent job of swallowing your shoes."

Danielle played through all her options, which included running away, and facing those she didn't want to face was nevertheless her best choice. Shit. A hundred times shit. Shit. Shit. Shit. Yeah, saying shit over and over in her mind wasn't helping. Time to pay the piper. Or face the piper, as the case may be.

Lifting one foot at a time, she pivoted on her toes to keep the ground from swallowing her shoes again, and almost turned right back around. One woman and two men stood in front of her. She recognized all three of them right away. There were few things in the world that lived up to anyone's expectations, the Grand Canyon being one, but Vixen somehow exceeded all of Danielle's expectations. The way she stood in the path, with a crooked smile and her palms on her hips, Vixen encompassed all the superheroes from the early days of comic books to the present flood of movies. Danielle figured the large, although large underplayed his sheer size, man standing beside Vixen with the smattering of gray in his hair was Bray, the man Vixen called mate. The third member of their welcoming party was the cowboy. Not that he was dressed as a cowboy now, but Danielle would have recognized his face in a sea of strangers.

Leighton.

Of all the members of Broken Peak Pack, he was the one she spent the most time fantasizing about in a totally not creepy way.

"For what it's worth, I don't believe anything I said. It's how I work. Gather all the data and give others the best of the information."

"The good news is you can go right to the source this time. The bad news is there's no one to give it to here, since everyone, well almost everyone, is a shifter and already possesses an intimate understanding of the subject matter." Vixen winked at her.

Actually winked. Danielle almost swooned at the gesture.

"We have a ways to go to get back to the Lodge, mind if we walk and talk?" Bray asked.

Danielle bobbed her head up and down. It was one thing to sit behind a desk in front of a bank of computer screens and peek into the lives of shifters, but standing in the presence of real live breathing shifters was something else altogether.

The General filed past Danielle and matched strides with Bray and Vixen further down the path.

Leighton leaned against a tree, crossed his arms over his massive chest, and tucked his hands under his armpits, while studying Danielle. The position of his arms lifted the bottom of his shirt, baring his defined stomach muscles. It didn't help matters that his worn jeans rode low on his hips. And it wasn't just the six pack, or maybe it was an eight pack. She didn't want him catching her staring at, but also the twin muscles that formed his Apollo's belt and pointed down.

Did shifters read minds?

She gulped and willed her mind to go blank. But then a hybrid version of the Stay-Puft Marshmallow man as the wolfman invaded her thoughts and lumbered around her brain.

Oh, God, this was bad. This was so bad.

Leighton combed his fingers through his light brown hair and shook his head from side-to-side. "You smell scared. You don't have to be scared of me. Of us."

Danielle let out a loud breath that was more huff than sigh. "I'm not scared."

He sniffed at the air. "Don't lie."

"Fine. You don't scare me." Danielle crossed her arms over her chest and stared at the ground between them.

Instead of erasing her investigation of the Pack like she should have, Danielle smuggled one of the files out of the Company. Leighton's file came home with her. When she couldn't sleep, she didn't listen to her podcasts. She read the few public records about him she managed to recover. Danielle memorized every broken bone, burn, and mark the doctors and nurses wrote down on his hospital records. And that his mother never brought him to the same hospital twice. Not to cover what appeared to be a history of abuse, but because they had a bigger secret to keep hidden. Then the records ceased. If Danielle didn't know any better, she would have guessed he died. Danielle had wanted to learn more about Leighton. But now that she was within arm's reach of him, she required a long shower to rinse away the film of shame from digging into his life.

Leighton didn't frighten her, that was the truth. The idea of him finding out she violated his privacy out of curiosity and would hate her for it scared the hell out of her.

She chanced lifting her head and meeting his intense stare. The power of his brilliant blue eyes was too much. His blue eyes turned silver and distant, and Danielle dropped her gaze.

"Come on, let's move." Leighton pushed off the tree and stuffed his hands deep in his pockets as he followed the others.

He didn't bother to stick around and see if she would follow. Of course, he wouldn't. Why would Leighton bother with a computer geek like her? Danielle needed to stop her daydreaming and concentrate on figuring out what happened next. She wasn't naive. She couldn't live with the pack for the rest of her life, so she had to spend what time she had here to establish a plan.

Danielle rushed after him, holding her arms out to the side so she wouldn't tip over. Stupid General. He could have offered her a chance to purchase a different pair of shoes. Something without a heel. "Um, Leighton?"

The star of her fantasies looked over his shoulder, but didn't stop, or even slow his pace. "What?"

Danielle needed to wave a wand and disappear what the shifters overheard. But since that was hopeless, she could at least make it better. "I just wanted to say, about what I said?"

"You sure you can walk and talk at the same time with those shoes?" He spun and walked backward along the trail.

Show off.

She halted, planted her hands on her hips, and stomped her foot. Any other location and the sequence of gestures would have performed flawlessly. In the middle of nowhere, off the beaten path — literally, and Danielle made an ass of herself flailing around like a fish out of water.

"So the answer's no." Leighton kept his hands in his pockets instead of coming to her aid. "Come on. At the rate you're moving, it'll be dark by the time we get back to the Lodge."

Danielle choked back a strangled curse, but Leighton had already swung back around and was striding away from her. He was nothing like the man she imagined. She had envisioned the shifters as sort of chauvinistic, but also chivalrous. However, Leighton hadn't helped her at all. He wasn't even willing to listen to an apology. Granted, she hadn't said she wanted to apologize, but he could have at least heard her out. Instead, he ridiculed and insulted her.

She did the only thing she could and stumbled after him, vowing that the first item she planned to acquire, once she decided where to go next, was a nice sturdy pair of boots.

Like the Grand Canyon, and unlike Leighton, the boots would live up to her expectations.

CHAPTER FOUR

LEIGHTON dug his hands deeper into his pockets and gripped the loose fabric. It was difficult walking next to Danielle and taking in her delicious scent, a blend of baking sugar cookies and cinnamon, while fighting the urge to reach out and touch her. The worst part about it was he wouldn't have recognized the smell of baking sugar cookies if Eleanor didn't bake cookies for Foster on the regular. If she didn't make those damn cookies, he'd never notice Danielle's scent. And if he hadn't been talking to Jackson about how he knew Eleanor was his mate, Leighton wouldn't have realized that the human woman currently struggling through the woods was his mate.

Well, that last part wasn't entirely accurate. His wolf made it abundantly obvious that the woman standing in the middle of the woods, in her flouncy skirt and ruffled blouse and high heels with her purple hair held back with little pink poofs, was all his.

Danielle didn't belong in the boondocks. She belonged in a big city with the shimmering colors around her eyes and the rosy pink of her lips. He was an ass for walking away from her and leaving her on her own, but he couldn't tether her to him and by extension Broken Peak. If he let her get even a little close to him, his wolf wouldn't need to claim her to bond with Danielle.

Bray slowed down enough to walk next to Leighton while Vixen and the old man went on down the trail.

"There a reason you aren't walking with the girl?"

Leighton stared straight ahead, "is this one of those rhetorical questions?"

"Vi brought you along with us to keep an eye on her. The girl is special to Vi and letting Danielle trip over every leaf and blade of grass isn't going to make Vi happy. And an unhappy Vi means I'm not happy either."

He took a deep breath, which was a colossal mistake because the scent of sugar cookies assaulted Leighton and his wolf went bonkers trying to burst out of his body. His wolf was already hard at work adding pressure to his feet, causing each step forward to be more challenging than the last. Leighton didn't even realize his wolf had that power.

Bray bumped his shoulder against Leighton's. The Alpha had learned long ago, when Mac first dropped Leighton off, that neither wolf nor boy enjoyed touching. Bray never forced it. Instead, he used bumps and leans in place of back pats and shoulder squeezes.

"She's important, this girl. Mac and Vi say so. I have no understanding how Danielle's expected to fit into our world, but even Eleanor found a reference to her in one of the old journals."

"The journals filled with gibberish?"

"Yeah, but if Mac and Vi both agree, we should probably defer to them. Vixen's griffin has some strange knowledge and when she chooses to share it with Vi, we need to take notice." Bray gave Leighton another shoulder bump, but this one had more force behind it and he faltered before catching his balance. "Besides, haven't you learned anything about women with Vi and El here? You don't intimidate them if they're scared."

"You're telling me I need to make it better, aren't you?"

"Either that or persuade the young woman not to tell Vi anything you said."

Leighton really was an asshole. He should have known better than using her fear to keep her away from him. But he didn't want hate to be why she stayed away. He could deal with her being scared. It pissed his wolf off that she was afraid of him, but it would piss both his wolf and him off if she despised him.

"Fine," Leighton grumbled.

"She's cute." Bray's gaze locked on Vixen walking ahead of them.

"Who?"

"The new girl. Who else?"

"Don't you already have a mate?" Leighton didn't appreciate Bray thinking of Danielle as cute. Not that he was in a place to do anything about it. It didn't matter if his wolf wanted Danielle, she deserved better than Broken Peak and she sure as hell deserved better than Leighton.

"Yep."

"So why mention she's cute?"

"The better question is why do you care if I think she's cute?"

Leighton should have let the subject drop. Bray led him right into the trap and both Leighton and his wolf followed along willingly. "Fine." Leighton growled and slowed the pace of his stride so Danielle could catch up.

Bray whistled a traditional bluegrass tune and loped up to Vixen and the General. The Alpha was altogether too satisfied with himself. As nice as some of the changes Vixen brought about in Bray were, the one where he became more involved in his pack's personal lives wasn't one of them.

Leighton wished he had something to give Danielle, a modest present to apologize. That's what both Bray and Jackson did when they pissed off their mates. Bray had a safe full of guns and knives wrapped with bows ready for the moment Vixen narrowed her eyes and got that expression on her face like she was going to let her griffin loose on him. And Jackson had everyone pick up any old book they encountered on their trips into town, just in case he did something stupid and Eleanor delivered her *I'm not angry, I'm disappointed* expression. But Leighton didn't know what Danielle liked, or if she'd even welcome a present after he'd been such a jerk. Too bad it was the beginning of November or he could have picked some flowers for her.

He peered over his shoulder, just to check how far back Danielle was and how much he needed to slow down for her to catch up. Not that he needed visual confirmation. The strength of her sugar cookie scent told him precisely how far away he was from her. She cautiously stepped along the trail with her arms hugged around her chest and held her gaze on the ground ahead of her. While he'd been speaking with Bray, she'd pulled her hair up on the top of her head, twisted it around into a sort of knot with two pencils sticking out of it. Too fucking cute.

"You might as well stop instead of slowing down or you'll be walking backward in a few minutes."

Leighton sighed and maintained a tight grip on his wolf. The beast was awfully close to the surface as it was and even if his wolf wouldn't hurt Danielle, he'd still scare her, which defeated the purpose of fixing things. Besides, if he concentrated on keeping his wolf in line, he ignored how fast his heart raced the closer she got to him.

He stopped and waited for her to catch up with him. As the bouquet of cookies grew stronger, Leighton laced his fingers behind his neck and stared up at the sky. He covered the various ways he could apologize. In the end, he opted for ripping the band-aid off and going for it. "I'm sorry."

"I'd probably do the same thing if I heard what I said." Her gaze remained on the ground, but at least Leighton could no longer detect fear lurking beneath her perfume.

"Do you honestly believe we're dangerous?" Leighton shoved his hands in his pockets before he wrapped his arm around her shoulder and pulled her against him, which would freak him out and send his wolf into a panic.

"No."

"Then why'd you say we are?"

"The unknown is always scary and scary things are always dangerous. Like snakes or spiders or high places without railings."

"Don't you mean dangerous things are scary?"

"It works in both directions."

"No it doesn't." Jackson growled and Danielle flinched at the noise. Shit, he was making matters worse. "We aren't dangerous. Not our pack. We might be a bunch of idiots, according to Bray, but we aren't a threat to anyone unless they come at us first. And whoever you're listening to, must not know the first thing about shifters if they call us skinwalkers."

"Oh my God, I knew it. Skinwalkers are real. See? There is always a kernel of truth in the conspiracy theories, you just have to dig it out. So, are the skinwalkers aliens? Because that's the current theory. I think."

"What? No. Maybe. I don't know if they exist. But legends have a way of becoming real lately." Leighton slowed his pace, so she didn't have to walk faster and risk tripping over her own feet on the uneven ground. "So you follow the conspiracy theories?"

"I don't follow them, not really, I just keep tabs on them. When the communities buzz with activity, it's generally a signal something is happening. Chances are, what has them running wild with assumptions isn't even related to what they assume is causing it. Well, except for the black helicopter brigade. Those guys are talented at coming up with almost accurate theories. Everyone else is about on par with the ghost in *Three Men and a Baby* or the munchkin hanging himself in *The Wizard of Oz*. Anyway, I can figure out what has them scrambling and frequently it's something we need to be concerned about. That's how I realized something was going on here. That skinwalker group went crazy about reports the government was suppressing…"

Danielle rambled on and Leighton half-listened while he studied the knot in her hair and the way it bounced as she walked. She was too fucking cute for Leighton's own good.

"… So I called the General, and he got in contact with Vixen. Then she showed up and had a few chats with some people, but I don't think they listened because a few days afterward the death notices crossed my desk. Crap-Damn it." Danielle stopped mid-stride with her foot hovering just above the ground.

"What?" Leighton sprang into action. Jumping in front of Danielle, he reached his arm out behind him to keep her there and stretched his other forward toward the unseen attacker that caused her to curse. "What's wrong?"

"Hampstead."

"Hampstead? Who's Hampstead?" Leighton pulled his arms back to his body and turned to her. His wolf pushed against him, demanding to break free so he could hunt down this Hampstead and rip his guts out.

"My hamster. He's almost four and, well, he's already lived past his predicted life span, and I can't abandon him to die now, but I can't call anyone to take care of him. Oh my God, I am the worst person alive, I left my hamster behind and now he's going to die a slow horrific death."

"I'll make sure he gets picked up and brought here." What was he thinking, besides not thinking? How the hell was Leighton going to locate anyone capable of breaking into her apartment and sneaking out with the hamster without *eating* the hamster.

"You will? Really? No, you don't have to. It's too much effort. I can't ask you to do that? You'd really do that for me." The words poured from Danielle's mouth a mile a minute.

She gave him the perfect opportunity to back out and if all the blood hadn't escaped his brain for other parts, he might have used it to get out of his offer. Instead, like the idiot Bray claimed they all were, Leighton doubled down. "Yep. We'll get him and bring him back here. I promise."

"Oh thank you, Leighton," Danielle threw herself at him and wrapped her arms around his waist while she pressed her cheek against his chest.

"I'm not doing it for you. I'm doing it for Vixen. She doesn't need you preoccupied with worries about a rodent." Leighton held his arms out to the side. The last thing he needed was to hug her. First, he didn't want to confuse his wolf, and second, Leighton didn't do hugs. He didn't do hugs or hand shakes or back pats. He didn't do touching.

Except at night. During the nightmares. And only because he was half-asleep when Vixen came into his room. Carefully, he reached down and gently pried her arms off him before taking a swift step backward. Instead of releasing both hands from her arms, he only dropped one. The other slipped down her arm to her wrist. "Come on, the others are too far ahead and Vixen will worry and circle back and then we'll get a dirty look."

"What? Oh, okay, sorry." Danielle didn't pull her wrist free as she followed behind him.

"So. Is Hampstead the only male in your life? Or do you have a boyfriend?" Leighton shouldn't have asked the question. It wasn't any of his business and learning if she left a male behind wouldn't alter the fact both he and his wolf needed to remain far away from her.

"No one current. Why?" She faltered on the uneven ground despite Leighton shortening his stride and slowing his pace to accommodate her shoes.

"Curious."

"Just curious?" Danielle picked up her knees and high-stepped across the ground, but that merely made her situation more problematic.

Leighton might be an asshole, but he wasn't a complete and total asshole. Pushing his wolf far enough down to prevent him from complicating matters, Leighton turned, scooped Danielle up before she could object, and swung her around to his back. If he carried her piggyback style instead of cradling her in his arms like he wanted, maybe it wouldn't destroy his wolf when he put distance between them back at the Lodge.

"Whoa! Warn a girl next time, why don't you?"

She squirmed against his back, and Jackson definitely wasn't thinking what it would feel like to wake up in the mornings with her clinging to him. "Hold on tight."

Once her arms tightened around his neck, he picked up his pace and jogged along the trail until they caught up with the others.

Bray glanced over his shoulder and raised an eyebrow, but said nothing. Leighton shook his head at his Alpha. Later. He'd deal with the questions later. It didn't dawn on Leighton until they crossed the front lawn of the Lodge and climbed the steps to the porch that not only was Danielle touching him, but he was also touching her. Their touching went beyond the accidental brushing against someone, but the contact didn't trouble either Leighton or his wolf. Fearful his wolf would push forward, Leighton let Danielle slide down his back, then strode away from her. The more distance he put between them, the better.

Vixen watched the entire spectacle with a curious expression. He'd seen it on her before when Eleanor arrived with her child, Foster. Great. Once his Alpha female got an idea in her head, she was like a dog with a bone and wouldn't give it up for any reason. Leighton was fairly confident the only reason Eleanor and Jackson finally mated was because they were tired of her constant meddling.

As long as Leighton stayed away from both Vixen and Danielle, Vixen wouldn't be able to interfere. Before Vixen roped Leighton into showing Danielle and the General where they'd be staying, Leighton escaped. With a sharp nod to Bray, Leighton turned and headed back down the stairs and across the grass to the woods. He'd give his wolf a chance to run and hopefully settle down.

"Leighton?" Vixen called from the porch.

"Let him go." Bray spoke at a normal volume, but Leighton heard the words and was grateful.

When he reached the forest line, he expected his wolf to push free like he normally did. Except his wolf was curled up and settling in for a nap. His beast didn't want to run.

CHAPTER FIVE

"WHERE can I set up?" Danielle didn't waste a second once Vixen showed her to the bedroom where Danielle would be staying. She removed her laptop and a small box of tools from her bag and perched on the edge of the bed while she unscrewed the back of her computer. "I'm going to need brand new computers. At least three. I'll give you the specs. And they have to be fresh out of the package."

Vixen leaned against the doorway and crossed her arms over her chest. It didn't matter how nice Vixen was to Danielle, the former de facto commander of Unit D, intimidated the hell out of her. Except that wasn't saying much. Vixen intimidated men in the special forces who faced death on a routine basis.

"I need to build an air-gapped network. As long as I'm the only one with access, I can keep it relatively secure. I presume you have security in place to notify you if anyone's in the area? We'll have to add a way to detect cell phone usage. It will be a pain, but I'll figure it out." When nerves hit Danielle, she babbled. Words gushed from her mouth in rapid succession, regardless if anyone nearby understood or even cared what she had to say. "Every computer that's ever been connected to the internet has to be yanked. We'll have to start fresh. I'll make a shopping list. We'll have to pay cash for them and have someone else buy them. Or several someones. You'll have to give them all instructions on how not to be detected."

"They know where we live, Danielle. Bray won't agree to moving, so there's no point in hiding our location. And we don't need an air-gapped network, we have you." Vixen pushed off the doorway and crossed the floor to sit on the bed. She reached for the laptop, removed it from Danielle's hands, and placed it between them. "Danielle, we didn't bring you here because we needed you, we brought you here because the Company has a habit of rewarding those associated with Unit D in not pleasant ways. I wasn't about to let anything happen to the woman who warned us about the Company's plans for Foster."

Danielle processed Vixen's words and when the meaning settled into her consciousness, she narrowed her eyes. "You decided?"

"The General and I decided, but Bray agreed. You helped us when it wasn't required and we don't leave any of ours behind."

"Wait," Danielle held up a finger. She needed a moment to consider what Vixen said before the woman moved on and Danielle lost the thread Vixen had dangled just out of Danielle's reach. "Your visit, it wasn't a warning was it?"

"I had rather low expectations they would heed my warnings."

"You wanted them to come after you, didn't you?"

"I reminded them I hadn't gone soft. That they came after me, in my house, is on them." Vixen reached down and squeezed Danielle's knee.

"We have an area set up just for you and your machines, but you don't need to worry about that right now. Let's introduce you to the others. They all want to meet you, especially a little guy who is still upset with me and Bray for not allowing him to come with us to greet you."

Danielle inhaled, preparing for what exactly, she had no idea, except everything Vixen said didn't fit with the script written in her mind and her go-to response had always been to fill up space with chatter. "So…"

"So, leave your computer, quit worrying about security and air gaps and networks and files for the rest of the evening, and come down to the kitchen with me to spend time with the others." Vixen's recommendation made perfect sense in a reasonable and rational world, but since Danielle learned about shifters, the world ceased being reasonable and rational.

She wiped her palms over the tops of her thighs and raised her leg to inspect her shoes. They'd seen better days, but they weren't in terrible condition. "Should I change?"

"Oh God, no. Those boys won't know what to do with you, and Eleanor and I need some fresh entertainment. There's only so many reasons you can use to persuade the guys they need to dress up as The Village People before they catch on." Vixen waved a hand in the air, much the way a queen waved to her subjects, "let's get a move on before the peanut gallery breaks past my guard and finds random imaginary chores to do outside your room."

When Danielle didn't stand swiftly enough for Vixen's satisfaction, she reached for Danielle's hand and tugged her to her feet. "Seriously though, Eleanor will only be able to hold them back for so long before they overwhelm her. They're becoming inoculated to her mommyisms."

"What's a mommyism?" Danielle thought she knew what Vixen meant, but had to ask anyway. Primarily to hear Vixen, the stone-cold assassin the government used for the missions with the smallest chance of success, explain the term. Plus, it was fun to hear Vixen say the word.

"It's a mix of her tone and counting. Wish I learned about the counting thing years ago. She doesn't even reach two and a half before they jump to her bidding. Though, they wait until I hit three."

"There's a rumor in Unit D that you were formed in a lab. I guess it started when someone wondered if you'd been hatched or were an alien. Anyway, the fact you don't know about the counting thing sort of ups the chance of hatching since I think if aliens did exist, they would use the counting technique. Every parent counts at some point in their lives. Usually when a kid is too big to be picked up, but too young to have any capacity to reason beyond asking why." Danielle's babbling returned in full force.

"None of the boys in the pack have any reasoning skills," Vixen went along with Danielle's rambling without a second glance and tugged her out the door. "Maybe that's why the counting thing is successful."

Nothing bothered Vixen, which helped Danielle not feel like a complete jerk for revealing that according to Unit D, the only two options for Vixen's origin were hatching and being an alien. At least Vixen's insistence they head to the kitchen kept Danielle from admitting that she didn't necessarily believe in the egg or alien theories, but hadn't entirely ruled out cloning and might have spent an afternoon sifting through the code worded files hoping to uncover something that explained Vixen's existence.

Standing in the entrance to the kitchen, Danielle pushed down the impulse to run back to D.C. as fast as her stiletto heels could carry her. Not that she would get far and based on the hike down the trail. There was also a definite chance of going ass over elbow and landing flat on her face, but at least then she wouldn't have five large men and one remarkably small woman gawking at her.

Wait. Not men. Males. That's what the transmits from Vixen called them. Males. And when in Rome...

Danielle scanned the faces of the males staring at her.

"This shouldn't be overly difficult. Finley and Tevin are the idiots in the shoving contest," Vixen gestured at two of the males who were indeed attempting to push each other down. "Allard is the one eating a sandwich like it's his last meal."

Allard waved his sandwich at Danielle before cramming the entire half into his mouth.

"You already met Bray."

The largest male of the group waved his spatula and turned back to the griddle on the stove top. "We're doing grilled cheese, which isn't so much grilled cheese as melts, since we add whatever sounds good to your sandwich. Let me know what you want and I'll make it for you."

"Grilled cheese is great." Danielle pressed her back against the doorjamb as both a means of support and a way to keep herself from fleeing the kitchen.

"Jackson and Eleanor," Vixen continued her introductions as though Bray hadn't interrupted. "And their son, Foster."

A little boy who looked like a miniature version of his father, slipped free from his mom's grasp and bolted across the floor before skidding to a halt in front of Vixen and Danielle.

"Hi. I'm Foster. Vivi said I had to stay here when she went to get you. I have a present for you. I wanted to put it in your room, but Mommy said I couldn't and had to wait in the kitchen for you. Do you like my shoes?" Foster's words sprung from his mouth in a spray of incoherent babbling.

Danielle, not having much experience with children, stared at him with wide eyes.

"Here," Foster held out a sheet of paper.

Danielle reached for it and flipped the paper over to view the drawing. A woman with dark hair, or at least Danielle thought it was a woman, stood in the middle of the page with two dogs, or maybe they were cats, standing on either side of her. One dog was bigger than the woman, but the other dog was much smaller.

"That's me," Foster pulled the sheet down so he could point to the smaller animal. "And that's Daddy and Mommy."

"Thank you." So they weren't dogs, but wolves. Good thing Danielle hadn't said something about dogs. She wasn't positive, but referring to the wolves as dogs probably wouldn't go over well with this bunch. Not that they'd cause her any harm, but Danielle could do without the dirty looks. "That's an amazing picture."

Finley, or maybe it was Tevin, they weren't related, but Danielle only had a few pictures to go by and confused them when they weren't dressed in their Halloween costumes of a construction worker and a leather aficionado, snorted.

"I can help you hang it on your wall." Foster jumped up and down in front of her.

"Of course, I'd love your help."

"Or we can put it on the fridge so you can share it," Vixen slid the picture from Danielle's hands and handed it back to Foster. "Go find a magnet and stick it to the door so we can all admire your masterpiece!"

Foster scampered off with the picture in hand to follow Vixen's recommendation.

"He's quite the artist, so you'll be receiving several more of these. He's also the resident curator and keeps track of every picture," Eleanor grinned at Danielle.

"Trust me when I tell you Vixen did you a favor. The boy has no comprehension of boundaries and would stroll into your room whenever he decides the picture needs changing." Jackson stared at Foster and gave a frustrated shake of his head. "And someone taught him to pick locks, so locking the door doesn't always stop him."

"Knowing how to pick a lock should be part of everyone's basic education. It's not my fault he's an apt student," Vixen grinned at Jackson. "Now, what do you want on your sandwich, Danielle?"

"Hmm? Oh, cheese is fine." Danielle looked behind her and down the empty corridor. Both Leighton and the General weren't in the kitchen, but Vixen hadn't remarked on their absence and Danielle didn't want to bring it up.

"Grab a seat. You can tell the boys what you did for the Company. They're dying to ask you loads of questions. I need to speak with the General and convince him to stick around for more than a day. I swear, that man's convinced the world will come to an end if he's not in the District to keep tabs on his network." Vixen gave Danielle a gentle shove toward the table. "Don't worry, you'll be fine."

Vixen spun on her heel and left Danielle alone in a room full of almost strangers. Well, at least she had the answer for where the General was.

The questions started almost instantly and Danielle spent the next hour answering them to the best of her ability. The good news was she answered most of the questions and managed not to inquire about Leighton once.

Though she definitely thought about him.

A lot.

CHAPTER SIX

LEIGHTON glared down at the empty cage. Less than five minutes before, a fat hamster that should not have had the capabilities to spring through the small opening on the top of the cage or the speed to dash across the floor and hide under the couch, sat happily on the wood shavings on the bottom of his cage.

This wasn't good. Hampstead escaping was the worst scenario. Well, okay, maybe not the worst, but damn close to the worst. The last thing Leighton wanted was to watch disappointment appear on Danielle's face when he told her he lost her hamster. The hamster he hadn't told her he was retrieving. He'd also have to admit to breaking into her apartment, but that required a different conversation because the woman took all the safeguards of the first victim in a horror movie. Frankly, it was a miracle someone hadn't broken into her apartment several times over.

She didn't even own an alarm! Didn't all humans have an alarm?

"Hampstead?" Leighton crouched down, pressing his fingertips against the hardwood floor and squinted under the couch. "Come on, boy. I have treats for you."

There weren't any treats, but the hamster didn't know that. Leighton wasn't even sure the hamster knew his own name.

"Come on, Hampstead," Leighton tapped his fingers against the floor.

The pack didn't own pets. Shifters and pets didn't mix well. Mostly because it was difficult to convince their animals not to eat the pets, but also because the pets perceived most shifters as predators. Rightfully so. Which was perhaps why Hampstead broke loose from his cage as soon as Leighton got close to him. Not that his wolf would eat the hamster.

Leighton's phone vibrated in his pocket and the sound of claws scratching across the wooden floor followed. Great. The rodent was on the move. Too bad Leighton hadn't planned ahead and placed pillows around the bottom of the couch so he could corral the little bugger back toward the cage.

The phone vibrated again and Leighton switched his phone off. How was he ever going to explain to Vixen or Bray why he drove off to the city in Eleanor's truck? What the hell was he thinking? Driving off would be easy to justify. It was how he was going to explain the hamster making a sudden arrival at the Lodge that would create the biggest problem.

None of that mattered though if he couldn't catch the fluffy escape artist.

Leighton pressed his cheek to the floor and searched beneath the furniture, looking for the slightest movement. He might have sharper senses than a human, but he'd have an easier time of it if the hamster moved. Unfortunately for Leighton, Hampstead might have been smarter than the average hamster.

CHAPTER SEVEN

IT WAS early. The sun wasn't even up. Not that Danielle could see since her room didn't have any windows, but the clock on the bedside table informed her it was a few minutes before six in the morning and the sun didn't rise until seven. She hated mornings. Not because she wasn't a morning person, she was agnostic regarding mornings or evenings. Danielle hated mornings because the frosty air waited to lambast her when she emerged from the pocket of warmth beneath the layers of blankets she heaped on top of her.

She closed her eyes and jerked the blanket over her head.

The alarm hadn't gone off.

Danielle made a habit of sleeping until the moment right before her alarm sounded. She hadn't set it the night before and she didn't have a phone to perform its vibrating dance across the table either.

What woke her up?

She pulled the blanket down and without her glasses squinted to see the foot of the bed, but found nothing. However, the soft noise of wood shavings rubbing against one another greeted her. She recognized that sound anywhere. After months of it waking her from a sound sleep in her apartment bedroom, she moved the cage to her living room.

Grabbing her glasses from the bedside table and slipping them on, she left the warmth of the blanket. Danielle scrambled out from under the covers and crawled down to the foot of the bed. There, on the floor, sat a small cage with her hamster inside cheerfully munching away on bite-sized pieces of apple.

"Hampstead!"

The little hamster paused his chewing and froze. She knew better than to open the cage. Hampstead took every opportunity to escape the confines of his cage. She was fairly certain he tested the strength of the wire bars when she wasn't around to witness it. Hampstead was tricky that way.

Danielle looked around the bedroom. She bit down on her bottom lip and peered at the closed door. Hampstead hadn't just materialized out of thin air. Someone had to have picked him up at her apartment. Either that or Leighton had done it himself. If Leighton had delivered Hampstead to her room, then he must still be close. Maybe she could find him and thank him before the rest of the house woke up?

Scooping the cage off the floor by its convenient handle, Danielle and Hampstead left her bedroom and headed down the hallway toward the kitchen. She chose the kitchen because it was the one place she knew she could find and wouldn't be wandering around aimlessly for someone to stumble across and then inquire why she was up and carrying a hamster in a cage.

As she rounded the corner and entered the dark kitchen, she spotted a broad shadow slouched over the kitchen table. Danielle jumped into the air with a yelp of surprise and clutched the cage to her chest. All at the same time. "Who's there?"

"Relax, it's just me."

Leighton.

She'd recognize his rough grumble anywhere, especially because of the way it did things to her body she wasn't willing to examine too closely just yet. Which was odd considering she heard his voice for the first time yesterday. "What are you doing here?"

"Well, to start, I'm having a bowl of cereal. But I live here, so it shouldn't be a surprise that you might find me in the kitchen. Do you want to put that down and join me, Dani?" Leighton lifted his chin toward the cage.

Dani. No one had ever shortened her name before. Usually because she didn't like it and corrected anyone who used a nickname instead of her given name. But with Leighton it was different. She enjoyed the sound of her abbreviated name coming from his lips. He could shorten her name as often as he liked and whenever he wanted, as far as she was concerned.

She placed the cage on the table and pushed it closer to the middle. There had been an incident when Hampstead banged against the base of the cage and moved it across the small table it rested on in an attempt to break free when the cage dropped to the floor.

"Did you pick him up for me?" Dani asked as she settled onto the chair across from Leighton's.

"No. I picked him up for Vixen's sake." Leighton answered without sarcasm as he pushed back from the table and crossed the floor to a cabinet where he removed a bowl and brought it with a spoon back to the table. "Frosted Flakes okay?"

He didn't wait for her response before pouring a pile of sugar coated flakes into the bottom of the bowl and adding milk.

Danielle picked up the spoon and beamed at the silent man across from her. Sure, Leighton had stated he'd find someone to pick up Hampstead, but she hadn't expected him to actually drive to D.C. and back in one night just to bring her a pet hamster. "How did you find my apartment and get into it?"

"You aren't the only one with tricks up their sleeves." He sat down and ate his cereal.

"Thank you. I hope it wasn't too much trouble."

"Not too bad," Leighton lied and Danielle knew it.

"You should have named him Houdini."

"Yeah, but I didn't realize he had mad escape skills until after I got him home, and I named him at the pet store. It seemed wrong to change his name after I called him Hampstead for a few weeks." She bit into a spoonful of frosted flakes and watched Hampstead munch on his fruit pieces so she wouldn't be tempted to stare at Leighton.

"He's a rodent. I don't think rodents learn names the same way other pets do." Leighton added more cereal and milk to his bowl.

Danielle shrugged. He was probably right.

They ate their cereal in companionable silence with Danielle sneaking glimpses at Leighton whenever she was positive he wasn't paying attention to her. The man, er male, wore a long-sleeved henley with the top three buttons undone. The shirt hugged his body perfectly, revealing the lines that defined his muscles. It should be criminal for a man to look that good. The ends of his light brown hair tickled at the collar of his shirt, and Danielle gripped the handle of the spoon to stop herself from running her fingers through the silky locks. Not that she knew whether his hair was soft. She just assumed. Leighton was the perfect combination of rugged handsomeness and tempting bad boy. He fit perfectly into her fantasy wheelhouse. Danielle needed to stay far away from him if she wanted to walk away from Broken Peak.

"Well, thank you for getting Hampstead for me. You probably think it's silly I worried about a hamster."

"I packed a bag of some of your clothes too. Since I was already at your apartment and chances are there won't be any more trips back to the city, I figured you might want a few of your own things."

Danielle leaned back in the chair and gaped at Leighton. Her initial thought was to clamber over the table and thank him with a giant hug. Her second thought went to the bottom drawer of her bedside table. Every woman had a drawer they hoped their parents never found and in cases of hospitalization or death had sworn a friend to a solemn vow to secure the items of said bottom drawer. Danielle didn't have one of those friends. She had the Company. If anything happened to her, they'd erase her entire existence.

The Company probably didn't have a contingency plan in place for clearing out that specific drawer if she ran away to an off-the-grid shifter compound and one of the smoking hot shifters broke into her apartment to recover her hamster and pack her a bag.

Those thoughts ran wild through her mind, but weren't appropriate to say aloud. She had to say something, though.

"Thank you." Danielle closed her eyes and stifled a groan. Thank you? That's what her brain came up with? Thank you?

"Welcome."

Maybe thank you wasn't charming or witty, but considering Leighton's response, they weren't the worst words to say.

Leighton and Danielle finished the rest of the early morning breakfast in a comfortable silence.

CHAPTER EIGHT

"ARE you sure you don't want to borrow a sweater or something?" Eleanor sat on the edge of the bed watching Danielle examine the odd selection of clothing hanging in the closet.

From the way Eleanor had been finding excuses to spend time with Danielle, she figured she had a new best friend. Or a first best friend. Not that Danielle minded. The idea of a best friend had always been something she considered, but never acted on. Between her job and a peculiar child who didn't have any of those great 80s movies moments, a best friend was always something she wished for but never experienced.

"Nope," Danielle popped the "p" in the word nope and fisted her hands on her hips.

Leighton had grabbed an odd selection of clothing: a pair of Ugg boots, khaki pants because she kept her jeans in drawers (Danielle assumed after he grabbed a handful of underwear and bras, he didn't want to venture into any other drawers), a weird combination of dressy tops, and a few dresses. Basically, what a kid would pack for Barbie if she was headed out on a trip where she had to dress up above the waist and be casual on the bottom. Her options amounted to the mullet version of wardrobes. The three pairs of high heels topped the fashion don't list residing in the closet. Not that she had many shoes to choose from, but she had a pair of loafers and ballet flats in her closet.

"I've made do with a lot less." Danielle selected the silver sequin tank, a knee-length black crochet sweater, and a pair of loose-fitting khaki pants. Vixen had declared that tonight was the last night they'd have an outdoor barbecue and insisted everyone, including some neighbors Danielle hadn't yet met, would be attending.

Sure, she'd be overdressed, but the sequined top was a better option than the silk blouses since most of them were close to transparent and her selection of bras were all dark. Yep, Danielle definitely had a current wardrobe that belonged to a forgotten Barbie who lost half her items over years of use.

If Danielle was being honest with herself, she picked the sequined tank top because it showed off the girls. She really didn't care all that much whether anyone identified the shade of her bra. She also picked out the top because she wanted Leighton to notice her. He had picked out this top from all the other tops in her closet. And as much as it was probably because Leighton grabbed the clothes within arm's reach, she wanted to believe he chose it because he liked it.

There. She said it. Not aloud, but she spoke those words to herself and made them as true as if she had said them to Eleanor.

"How do I look?" Danielle tucked the cuffs of her pants into her boots and spun for Eleanor.

"Gooooood?" Eleanor dragged out the word and lifted the tone of the last few letters as though she was asking a question.

"Well, it was this sweater and tank or four blouses because they're all summer wear."

"Yeah, if it's not denim or flannel, the boys are pretty much hopeless." Eleanor leaned forward and rested her elbows on her knees. "I'm sure I have a sweater you can borrow, or we can ask Vixen?"

Danielle looked down at her chest and cupped her breasts while staring unabashedly at Eleanor's chest. "You're like half my size and my girls are twice as big as both yours and Vixen's combined." She dropped her arms and looked up at Eleanor's face with a grin. "At least I have a pair of boots."

Eleanor hopped to her feet and returned the infectious grin. "It's only fair for you to make Leighton dress up in his cowboy costume until the clothes Vixen ordered arrive."

Danielle's nose scrunched up as her grin grew. "He looked good in that costume."

"Come on. I know you think there's a lot of food, but when those boys get together to eat, the food goes fast. Plus, Roose will join us and he eats like a, well, like a bear actually." Eleanor threaded her arm through Danielle's and pulled her out the door and down the hallway.

Halfway to the front door, the butterflies in Danielle's stomach somersaulted and back-flipped. Stopping and running back to her room wasn't an option with Eleanor holding her arm. For such a tiny woman, Eleanor sure was strong. She probably did pull-ups while hanging off one of Jackson's massive biceps. Or perhaps she got her muscles from keeping hold of Foster. Danielle wrangled her wandering thoughts back under control and tugged down the back of her tank with her free hand. No reason to accidentally flash the girls to the entire pack and their friends because she tripped while her mind ran off on a Leighton tangent.

Danielle and Eleanor stepped out onto the front porch. Once more, Danielle wanted to run back to her room in hopes the butterflies and nerves might settle down enough to keep her mind from wandering off to relive the fantasies she had created about the pack. One member in particular.

Vixen and the General stood in the middle of the large yard and stared out into the dark expanse of the forest while Bray and Jackson argued over the correct way to grill steaks and the rest of the pack lounged at the picnic table next to the huge bonfire built off to the side. Well, all except for Foster. He ran laps around the yard, circling the picnic table and fire pit before arcing around Vixen and the General, then Bray and Jackson in a mutated figure eight made of three loops instead of two.

Where were all these nerves coming from? She wasn't this nervous when she and the General pulled into the clearing and walked down the trail to the Broken Peak Pack. She took a deep breath and walked down the few steps to the ground. Thank God for Eleanor standing next to Danielle and keeping her upright since her gaze locked right on Leighton and she couldn't pull herself together enough to not stare like a gibbering idiot at him.

"Hi." Danielle waved. She might have spoken the word to everyone, but she intended it for Leighton. She might have even said Leighton's name to herself.

Crud.

She needed to work on not thinking things since she still wasn't convinced shifters didn't have the power to read minds.

Eleanor wrapped her hand around Danielle's elbow and led her across the yard to the picnic table Vixen ordered from Amazon. Apparently, there wasn't anything that couldn't be ordered from the mega online store. Eleanor gave Danielle a gentle shove to the table before intercepting her son on his next lap.

"Really? None of you stopped to think a kid shouldn't be running around a hot grill or fire?" Eleanor kept a tight grip on the back of Foster's shirt, preventing him from returning to his laps.

Six males stared up at Eleanor with wide-open eyes and dropped jaws.

Nope.

None of them had considered the risks. The General and Vixen weren't any better with the way they stared out into the forest and ignored Eleanor's chastisement.

Eleanor continued with her lecture, but all Danielle heard was a dull hum as she settled onto the bench across from Leighton. It was difficult to pay attention to what Eleanor was saying when the sight of Leighton dressed in a worn flannel shirt with the sleeves rolled up to his elbows and the collar unbuttoned enough to display a hint of chest hair tempted Danielle's vision. She couldn't decide what was better, the scruff of a day-old beard on his jawline, the dusting of light hair on his arms and chest, or the way his hair hung down over his face as he bent over the table, holding a mason jar of moonshine between his hands.

"Um, hey, Leighton. Thanks again for picking up Hampstead." Danielle's brain was so preoccupied with the vision in front of her it ceased being capable of forming a cogent sentence. She cleared her throat and yanked her brain back in gear. "I know he's just a hamster, but it meant a lot. With everything that's happened and probably will happen, it's nice to have something familiar around. You know?"

Leighton turned his attention away from Eleanor and focused it entirely on Danielle. The intensity of his stare was so powerful, she nearly fell backwards off the bench to avoid his scrutiny. She would have run back into the lodge and hid beneath her bed, if Leighton's stare didn't also hold some secret power to keep her frozen in place.

He could ignore her and pretend she wasn't anything more than a visitor all he wanted, but Danielle didn't buy his act. If she hadn't been staring at his eyes, she would have missed it. His eyes flashed silver with a glow that wasn't found on human eyes. His wolf was close. Just for a minute and then the glow faded away and the cool blue irises returned. She might have believed she had imagined it, with the darkness of night settling in and thee light from the fire, except she saw that bright silver once before. The first time she had been face to face with Leighton and he'd overheard her spiel about shifters being dangerous.

Danielle dropped her elbow to the table and rested her chin on her palm. What if her initial assumption that the silver appeared because she made Leighton angry was all wrong?

"Is this the one Vixen keeps talking about?" A low booming voice grumbled from behind her.

Danielle snapped her head around and nearly fell off the bench as she leaned back to take in the enormous man now standing behind her. She hadn't heard a thing. Where had that giant of a man come from? She was so busy staring at the blond behemoth, that she stopped thinking about Leighton and what his glowing eyes meant. It shouldn't be possible for anyone to be larger than the males she had met in person since arriving at Broken Peak, but this particular male blew that belief out of the water.

The giant crossed his arms over his chest. Danielle noted his forearms were bigger than her thighs, not an easy feat considering most of the men she'd spent any time with usually had thighs smaller than hers. "Vixen says you're going to help us. Are you?"

An old man with a gray grizzled beard and matching eyebrows stepped out from behind the giant just as Foster broke free from his mother's grasp and flung himself at the giant. "Don't be rude, Roose. Let's wait for Leighton to introduce us before we interrogate the poor lass."

Danielle straightened her neck before she developed a permanent crick and grinned at the old man. She recognized both males from the pictures she'd stolen from the General and Vixen's correspondence. Vixen hadn't used names, and Danielle didn't know if they were wolves or something else, but they were friends with Broken Peak Pack and Vixen, which made them friends with Danielle in an odd way.

"Dani, meet Mac, the old coot, and Roose." Leighton growled from beside her. At some point, Leighton changed seats and now sat next to her.

How had that happened?

"Oh my gosh, you can teleport!" Her words slipped free from her thoughts.

"What?" Leighton, Finley, Foster, Allard, and Roose all spoke at the same time and stared at Danielle as though she had sprouted a fifth and sixth head.

Mac bent over, clutching his stomach and laughing louder than necessary. He wheezed out an explanation between guffaws. "Nope, lass, we're just good at not making much noise unless we want to and your hearing ain't nearly as keen as our kind."

Roose lowered his eyebrows as he stared down at Danielle. He looked over at Leighton while extending his mammoth hand to her. "Nice to meet you."

Danielle reached for his hand on instinct and shook, figuring that was his intention, except her fingers couldn't even wrap around his palm. Roose's fingers loosely held hers as he lifted her arm up and down. If he wasn't being careful, he could have dislocated her shoulder.

Or maybe even rip her arm out.

"You are huge. Do you know that?" Danielle asked.

"Forgive her, Roose. She doesn't have a filter. Not that anyone else here has one either, but you can always trust that Danielle will tell you exactly what she's thinking." Vixen glanced over at the picnic table and winked.

"Well then, with introductions out of the way, can I tempt you with a jar of some 'shine?" Mac held up an earthenware jug and waved it in the air.

Before Danielle uttered a word, a jar filled with light yellow liquid appeared in front of her face. Her gaze moved from the jar of what Danielle assumed was liquor to the face of the man holding it.

"Already taken care of." Leighton grinned at Mac, baring his teeth.

Mac chuckled. "You don't say."

Danielle looked between Leighton, the male who had invaded her thoughts since the first time she looked at a grainy photo of him, and the old man. Whatever was happening between them, she didn't think moonshine had anything to do with it.

"Is that paw-paw, Leighton?" Eleanor called over from the grill where she was standing next to Jackson and poking him in the ribs with her elbow. "I want a glass. Why didn't you offer me some, Jackson?"

Jackson closed his eyes and shook his head from side to side. "Because, woman, you were still going on about not letting our boy tear around like a boy and didn't let me get a word in."

Leighton put his hand on Danielle's back and guided her around so she was once more facing the table. Mac and Roose, with Foster hanging off his back, sat down at the table with the others. Shortly after, Vixen and the General made their way over.

While everyone shifted around to make room for each other, Leighton bent his head down so his lips barely brushed against Danielle's ear. "I like your shirt. It's pretty and shiny."

"And silver. Like your eyes sometimes." Danielle's eyes widened as the words spilled out of her mouth. She hadn't meant to say that. To stop any more thoughts from forming into words, she swallowed down a huge gulp of the drink in her hand and nearly coughed it back up. She wiped the back of her hand across her lips. "Strong."

Everyone sitting at the table stared at her, watching to see what she'd do next. There was only one way to respond. Perhaps, if she had stopped to consider the consequences, she would have put the jar down and made a crack about being a lightweight. But she didn't. Instead, she lifted the jar to her lips, tilted her head back and swallowed the entire contents in a few long gulps.

The one bright spot of her not well-thought out plan was by drinking the moonshine so quickly, the alcohol somehow entered her bloodstream and numbed her mind before it burned her throat and caused more coughing.

Her performance didn't stop the staring. In fact, now Bray, Jackson, and Eleanor were also staring at her.

"What?" Danielle hiccuped.

"Well, she can still speak." Someone said.

Danielle couldn't place the voice with a face or name. Probably because her eyes stopped working. The world around her had turned fuzzy. Like when people talked about TV before cable and had to adjust antennas to get a clear picture.

"And she hasn't fallen over yet."

"Quick. Someone give her food. It will sop up some of the booze."

"I don't think what was in that jar qualifies as booze." Danielle hiccuped again.

"And there goes her speech."

"Eat this, Dani." A hamburger pushed against her mouth until she opened it and took a bite. "Chew it. Nice and easy now. Take your time before you swallow."

A warm hand rubbed small circles on her back as she followed the orders.

God, it was so good. It wasn't right for a burger to taste as good as the one she was eating. They must have laced it with some magic.

Laughter greeted her ears, but she didn't care. Everyone could have been screaming about the end of the world and it wouldn't have mattered. Not with the perfect hamburger in front of her. When the hamburger disappeared from the hand holding it, she looked around the table at the blurry faces.

"Who took it?"

Vixen leaned across the table and grinned at Danielle. "Took what?"

"My burger." Danielle lifted the hand and turned it about, looking for her hidden hamburger.

"Maybe the burgers are magic. Her words are coming back. Leighton, quick, give her another one."

She spotted the bun at the same time the aroma of grilled meat hit her nose and stretched her arms across the table. Something must have been off with her equilibrium, because she fell to the side, right into the wall of muscle next to her. Instead of bouncing away, a muscular arm wrapped around her waist and pulled her closer. Danielle's body tried to jostle some sense back into her brain. The butterflies in her belly, which until then had been quiet, dipped lower, sending a tingling jolt between her legs.

Slamming her legs together to get the butterflies under control, Danielle snatched the hamburger from Leighton's hands and bit into it. If she kept her mouth occupied with food, she couldn't say anything stupid, like how he made things all tingly and shorted out her brain.

A glass of water, or at least she thought it was water, appeared on the table in front of her.

"Drink it up, Dani." Leighton whispered in her ear and his breath tickled her ear.

A shiver ran through her body, but it didn't cool her down in the slightest. Apparently, moonshine made Danielle hot. Or maybe Leighton's closeness raised her temperature.

"Why do I need water?"

"Because you'll have a headache tomorrow whether or not you drink the water, but it'll be a hell of a lot worse if you don't." Eleanor answered her question with a lift of her own water. "I use the sip of Mac's shine then a glass of water approach to keep the pains of a hangover at bay. Vixen does the boot and rally. Really, anything that either dilutes or removes the alcohol is a decent tactic."

"Don't worry. I won't let anything bad happen to you." Leighton's words rumbled around the table and enveloped her like a warm blanket.

Danielle tried to pretend his words didn't have any effect and failed miserably. His voice danced down her spine like a light fingertip tickling her skin.

The others pretended not to hear what Leighton said or how Danielle responded and returned to their own conversations and the food on their plates.

Leighton spooned all the sides, set in the middle of the table, on to a plate then placed a hamburger on it as well before setting it down in front of Danielle. Her eyes bugged out at all the food. She already inhaled two burgers and didn't need any more food, except she wanted it.

Everything tasted amazing. Yeah, the moonshine might have played a role, but she didn't think it was the only reason. She leaned back on the bench, forgetting for a moment there wasn't a back to keep her from falling off. Before she tilted back more than a few inches, Leighton's arm was behind her, keeping her safe.

Not letting anything bad happen to her.

Just like he promised.

Danielle pressed her palm against her stomach and leaned back against Leighton's arm, gratefully accepting his support. "Ugh, I'm going to have to work out."

General Jesup snorted. "There's no gym, Ms. Howe. If you want to work out, you'll have to take a run through these woods." He waved his hand behind him at the mass of dark trees providing a protective wall around the yard in front of the house.

She rolled her eyes at the old man. He knew better. Even if the pack had a gym hidden away somewhere, she still wouldn't use it. Danielle didn't even use the gym in her apartment building.

Vixen smirked and leveled her steady gaze on Danielle. "I told you we didn't bring you here because of your computer skills, but the General and I have been talking."

"About?" Leighton asked before Danielle could even get her mouth open and the word out.

Vixen and Bray shared a look, but Danielle was clueless to what it meant. They looked at each other for a few seconds before Bray gave Vixen a sharp nod and picked his hamburger back up. If anyone else sitting around the table noticed the silent communication, they didn't comment.

Vixen released a lengthy breath and continued speaking, ignoring Leighton's question. "I have a project for you. It's likely to be impossible, but there's a reason the Company snatched you away from the DOJ's grasp. If anyone can implement it, you can. We'll talk more about it tomorrow, but don't make any plans for the morning."

Danielle laughed. What Vixen said wasn't funny, but it reminded Danielle of the absurdity of her situation. She could have laughed or cried, and Danielle opted for laughing. Once she caught her breath, she looked up at Vixen. "What other plans would I possibly have?"

"You never know." Vixen gave her a knowing smile then lifted her jar of liquor up at Bray. "To bootin' and rallyin' tonight."

"You know that's not a nice toast, right?" Roose asked, holding a burger a few inches away from his mouth. "And it's really not a pleasant thing to say while everyone's eating."

"Oh please." Finley shoved a forkful of potato salad into his mouth. "I've seen you eat things that would cause the rest of us to boot 'n rally."

"Not on two legs, you haven't." Roose put the burger back on his plate and glared at Finley.

"Enough." Mac, Bray, and the General all spoke at once.

Vixen reached behind Finley and squeezed Bray's forearm. "There's still another plate of burgers that won't eat themselves and Eleanor and I don't want to be forcing everyone to eat leftovers, so finish up the beans, slaw, and salads."

It was about that same time when Leighton must have realized that not only was his arm wrapped around Danielle's waist, but his hand was squeezing the flesh of her hip. He had been applying just enough pressure for her to slide closer to him one millimeter at a time.

Leighton snatched his arm back and dropped his hand to his lap. The movement was enough to attract Danielle, and she glanced down at his lap.

Unbelievable.

He was hard. Or at least Danielle hoped he was hard, because if he wasn't, it meant his dick was on the giant size of large.

If Danielle was being honest with herself, it wasn't as though she was unaffected by his touch either. Except Leighton had made it abundantly clear that everything he was doing was because it helped Vixen and not because it made Danielle happy.

Asshole.

Danielle needed to get away from everything. She couldn't sit at the table next to Leighton, with the others pretending not to look at them any longer.

"Excuse me a moment." She scrambled over the bench and almost landed on the ground in an ungraceful heap, but Leighton's hand steadied her before she planted face first into the grass.

CHAPTER NINE

FOSTER opened his mouth and Eleanor reached across to cover it before he said anything. She turned to Vixen and tilted her head at Danielle's slow retreat across the yard. Vixen shook her head and Bray glared at Leighton.

"Yeah, yeah. You don't have to tell me. I know."

"Foster, stop licking my hand." Eleanor uncovered the pup's mouth once Danielle was far enough away not to hear the question Foster was about to ask.

"What don't you have to tell Uncle Leighton? And where is Dan-Dan going?"

"How come I don't get a cool nickname like Vixen and Danielle, Foster?" Finley did his best to distract the pup.

"I don't know." Foster shrugged, then dug into his pocket and pulled out a toy car. One of several that Vixen, Mac, and Roose always seemed to be giving him after a trip to town. "If she doesn't feel good, I'll share my car. This one always makes me feel better."

Allard chuckled. "Don't worry, kid, She'll be feeling a whole lot better in a little while."

Both Vixen and Eleanor delivered a healthy smack to whatever part of Allard they could reach.

"Ow!" Finley rubbed his shoulder where Vixen hit him instead of Allard. "What was that for?"

"Do you have a car you can share with her, Uncle Leighton? You can have mine." Foster attempted to break out of his father's grasp, but failed when Roose's large hand came down on his shoulder and helped keep Foster at the table.

Leighton swung his legs over the bench and stood, then hurried after Danielle who was zig-zagging her way across the yard to the woods.

"Oh, he has something he wants to share all right." Allard snickered and high-fived Finley, who received two more back-handed smacks.

"What? I didn't say anything!" Finley rubbed his other shoulder.

"You were thinking it." Jackson glowered and did his best not to laugh. "The kid repeats everything, but you were betting on that. Call it a preemptive move to keep you from opening your mouth in front of Leighton and getting the crap beat out of you."

"Mommy! Daddy said crap. He needs to put a quarter in the jar!"

Eleanor buried her face in her hands and shook her head in defeat. But at least with the chaos around the picnic table, no one had sneaked after Leighton and Danielle to spy on them.

"Dani, wait up!" Leighton called to the most frustrating woman he'd ever met, but she ignored him. Which only made him more frustrated. "Damn it, Dani!"

She came to a sudden halt and whirled on her heel, but never considered the amount of alcohol still flying through her body and swayed on her feet. Leighton wasn't close enough to prevent her from tipping over. Her arms wind milled, and she leaned precariously forward before overcompensating and landing on her adorably heart-shaped ass with an equally adorable unladylike grunt.

"Stop moving around so much."

"I'm not moving." Leighton offered his hand, but she ignored it.

Leaning back on her arms, she scowled up at him and pursed her lips together.

He'd been where she was before. They all had. Mac's moonshine was strong enough to flatten a shifter, whose metabolisms ran fast enough to burn through most store-bought alcohol that made getting drunk virtually impossible. Leighton couldn't imagine what Danielle was going through, but it couldn't have been pleasant.

Instead of demanding she stand up with him, he sat on the ground next to her. But not too close. Sitting too close caused all tonight's complications.

Except, right at that moment, Dani blew her bright purple bangs from her eyes and Leighton's stare never moved from her lips. He'd been doing an excellent job of not staring at her mouth since she first appeared, but now, with none of his pack around him, he gave in. He brought his hand to her chin and turned her face until she looked at him.

"You're going to be trouble, Dani, do you know that?"

"What do you mean I'm going to be trouble? You're the one who's making all the trouble." Her words came out as a jumbled mess.

Dani was about to try again when he ran his thumb across her bottom lip before leaning forward and brushing his mouth against her soft lips. She stiffened for all of five seconds before her body softened against his. His palm drifted from her cheek to the back of her neck and he held her head where he wanted it. He leaned over her and brushed his tongue against her lips until she parted them for him.

Danielle moaned, giving him access to her mouth as he drew her into his lap before drawing away from her with a low growl. "You're drunk, Dani, and as much as I'd love to see just how wet you are and if you taste as good as you smell, I don't do drunk girls."

Apparently, Leighton said the worst possible combination of words because she didn't bother to wait for her eyes to focus before she raised her hand and brought her palm down hard on his shoulder. Dani snapped her hand back and shook it as though it stung.

"Ow!" Dani stared down at her palm. "You hurt me."

"No. You hurt yourself. If you hadn't tried to slap me, your hand wouldn't hurt."

Dani pushed against his chest to separate herself from his lap. He should have let her go, but Leighton worried she'd hurt herself even more on her own.

"What you said hurt me."

"What? That I don't do drunk girls? Why is that a hurtful thing?"

"Because. You kissed me. And you gave me Mac's moonshine knowing I'd probably get drunk. And then you said what you did." Dani looked down at the ground, avoiding Leighton's eyes.

"Dani, the last thing you need is a fling with me. Sure, you might want it, but you don't need it."

"How about you let me decide what I need. I'm a grown woman, Leighton. I've been making my own decisions for a few years now."

"And where did that get you? On the run from a kill squad and hiding in pack land with a bunch of idiot shifters who didn't have anywhere else to go but here. Broken Peak Pack is like the island of the misfit toys. It's the last resort before we're put down or banished."

Leighton hadn't planned on sharing that much about his pack. Having an Alpha female might have made the pack balance a little better, but the pack was still filled with fuck ups. Hell, even Foster was a mini misfit with his uncontrollable shifts and a wolf pup that hated ceding control back to the boy. The last thing Dani needed was an attachment, even if it was superficial, to Leighton or the pack.

And if she hated him, all the better for her, it would make it easier for her to move on. Leighton and his wolf might be broken, but he wouldn't let Dani break.

Dani pressed her palms against his chest and pushed back while twisting her shoulders in another attempt to break free.

"Dani. Wait."

"No. Let me go, Leighton. You're mean. And you're mean."

She swiveled in his lap again, making his life all the more difficult because all her squirming wasn't helping the state of his hard dick. His erection hadn't gone away since it made its presence known when he sat next to her at the picnic table. If anything, his dick got harder.

Fucking hell.

"Dani. Stop." He tightened his arms around her and pulled her close. "I'm sorry. Okay?"

"No. Not okay." She had stopped squirming while Leighton was talking, but went right back to wiggling around as the words left her mouth. "Ever since Vixen left the Company, I've been watching you all from a distance. For every picture, I've created a story about everything that happened right before and after that frozen moment in time. And now, now that I'm here, I can finally not just be an observer, but a participant. I get to be part of the story. And then, you go and do something that's even better than I imagined with that kiss, but ruined it by opening your mouth and saying something stupid. Sorry doesn't fix it. Sorry can't erase that kiss. Sorry can't take away the hurt of you doing one thing but constantly reminding me it has nothing to do with me. And then kissing me. Like that. Like it means something. But the next words out of your mouth is about not doing drunk girls!"

Danielle flailed her arms as the words rushed from her mouth. Leighton did his best to avoid her arms and hands, and was mostly successful, but dodging her words and the hurt and anger behind him was hopeless. His wolf didn't get off unscathed either. The beast was busy shredding his insides because of Dani's pain.

Leighton closed his eyes and took a deep breath. Dani had said so much and he didn't know where to begin. And what was that comment about their kiss being better than she imagined? She had no business imagining anything with him, most of all a kiss. But right then wasn't the time or place to have that discussion about bonds and claimings. Plus, he wasn't the best one to have that conversation with her. Maybe Eleanor could talk with Dani and set her straight.

In the meantime, he did his best. "I can't give you anything else, Dani. What I can give you won't be enough and when I can't give you anything more, you'll hate me more than you do now."

Danielle wiped the back of her hand across her nose. "I don't hate you, Leighton. I don't especially like you at the moment, but I don't hate you."

"Well, my wolf sure as hell thinks you hate me and is punishing me."

Danielle turned in his lap and pressed her hands against his cheeks, holding his head in place so she looked in his eyes. "Is he there? Inside?"

Leighton's blue eyes flashed silver and the corner of Danielle's mouth lifted in a slight smile.

"There you are. Stop punishing Leighton. I'm a big girl and I can take care of myself."

Both Leighton and his wolf growled together. If he was lucky, Dani would think the noise came from the beast and not the man.

"And you." Dani narrowed her eyes and pursed her lips. "The General yanked me out of my world and dumped me into yours, so I'm here now and not going anywhere in the foreseeable future. You have to work this out sooner or later, Leighton, because I can't exist in limbo trying to interpret what you really mean when you do something nice." She pressed her forehead against his and closed her eyes. "If you aren't careful, you're going to lose me before you've even had a chance to have me."

Danielle pushed off his lap and stood up with a wobble. She walked away from him without a backwards glance or another word.

His wolf whined at her departure, but didn't shred Leighton up from the inside like he had been doing.

The wolf obeyed Dani's command to stop punishing Leighton. Before Leighton thought too much about the why of the beast's shift in attitude, Leighton jumped to his feet and followed after Dani.

He wasn't worried about anything that might be in the woods hurting her. Leighton was more anxious about her falling over a small branch or a root. He remembered how she struggled hiking down the trail to the Lodge when she first arrived and she didn't have any of Mac's moonshine in her at the time. With the amount she had drunk and the way her body lurched from side to side as she huffed off, Leighton was concerned a blade of grass could take her down.

CHAPTER TEN

DANIELLE hugged herself as she reached the edge of the woods. Granted, her arms weren't a satisfactory replacement for Leighton's arms, but she'd make an ass of herself if she spent any more time with him considering how hard the moonshine hit her.

Forget sodium pentothal, the Company needed to use some of Mac's moonshine instead. She hadn't been able to block the words from spilling out of her mouth. The last thing she needed was to blurt out everything in the presence of the rest of the pack, hence the rapid escape to the woods.

What if she had revealed even half of what she told Leighton while sitting with the others? She didn't want to chance not being sober enough to shut her trap before she listed all her sins. Sins like digging into Leighton's history.

The even cadence of heavy footsteps approached from behind.

She didn't need to look over her shoulder to confirm it was Leighton. Probably following her because Vixen would get angry with him if Danielle got lost.

Stupid Vixen.

No. That wasn't fair. Not stupid Vixen. Stupid Leighton.

"Dani, wait up."

She didn't look back, but waved a hand and kept right on walking. She had no clue where she was going, but she needed to get as far away from stupid Leighton as possible.

"C'mon, Dani, I wanna talk."

"Well, I don't want to talk. Besides, we did all our talking already, remember?"

Leighton caught up and fell into step with her, but kept enough space for a third person to walk between them. "Dani, I don't touch people. Not because I don't want to, but because my wolf doesn't like me getting close to anyone."

Danielle stopped and faced him. She lifted her chin in what might have been a show of defiance, or so she could see into his eyes. She wasn't sure which, but both worked for the situation. "Go on."

"Before Vixen, my wolf was as likely to attack a pack member as he was to play with them. I kept my distance from everyone and everyone kept away from me. Even Bray didn't ask too many questions when I changed on my own."

"Okay?" Danielle crossed her arms over her chest. "And why are you telling me all this?"

"Fuck, Dani, I don't know." Leighton combed his fingers through his hair, pushing it out of his eyes. "Just that before you, I wouldn't have let anyone touch me, and I sure as hell wouldn't have touched someone. Or kissed them."

"You've never kissed someone?" She didn't believe a male who looked like Leighton didn't have a ton of women, and men too for that matter, fawning all over him when he left pack territory.

"Not like I kissed you, no. I don't do relationships, Dani. It isn't by choice and it isn't some excuse. My wolf can't deal with a relationship. But for whatever reason, he doesn't get angry around you."

"But what does that mean, Leighton?"

"It means that I'm going to do a lot of things that will piss you off and make you angry, but I don't mean to. I just don't know any better." Leighton sighed and looked up at the star-filled sky. "Plus you're a human."

"You say that like it's a bad thing, except *I* was the one to make sure Vixen learned about the Company's plans for Foster. And *I* also gave her enough information to escape the assassination team assigned to eliminate her. Me, a puny little human." Dani poked a finger at his chest. Cripes, he was built. Poking him was like poking a brick wall. "I'm a loyal friend, even if I am human and Foster and Vixen aren't. Now, if you'll excuse me, I need to stomp off so I can be alone and think."

"Dani, I can't let you go off alone. My wolf won't allow it. Let me walk with you and I promise I won't say a word?"

Danielle blew her hair out of her eyes and considered his words. Apparently she didn't answer fast enough for Leighton's taste. He shoved his hands in his pockets and bumped his shoulder against hers.

"I'm just going to follow you, anyway."

"You won't say a word?"

Leighton crossed his pointer and middle fingers over his heart. "Fine."

She resumed her stomping and Leighton stepped along with her. Ten minutes later and Danielle didn't feel any better. Plus, she was sure she was lost and had no clue how to find her way back to the house.

"It's not just my wolf." Leighton stared straight ahead and spoke just above a whisper.

At first, she almost reminded him he promised to be quiet, but something about the pleading tone of his voice convinced Danielle whatever he had to say he hadn't said to anyone else before.

"I'm not good at the relationship thing either." Leighton took her silence to be the invitation it was and continued. "Even if my wolf didn't make my life miserable, I don't do relationships. It's not just my wolf that isn't capable, I can't do it either."

Danielle didn't have any words for his admission. Not that Leighton expected them, but sometimes it was nice to be heard. She opted for a noise that offered no opinion and didn't make any commitments. "Hmm."

"My parents. It wasn't good. Not like Vixen and Bray, or even Jackson and Eleanor. And my father definitely wasn't a good mate. He sucked as a father, but he was even worse as a mate. Our Alpha, he didn't have much control of the pack. It was a shitshow and our family had a starring role."

"You aren't your father, Leighton." Danielle didn't know the details, but she had put two and two together from the files.

"But what if a part of whatever made him what he was is inside me, is part of my wolf? I can't let you take that ri–"

A loud pop came from Danielle's left. Before she even turned to see where the noise came from, Leighton jumped on top of her and yanked her to the ground beneath the shelter of some prickly bushes. Several more pops followed the first, but Danielle couldn't even move her head. Leighton shielded her from whoever was shooting at them with his body.

She twisted her head to the side, if only so she wasn't breathing in dirt, but knew better than to lift her head. Danielle hadn't realized she was saying anything at all, much less repeating the phrase *oh my God* over and over until Leighton shushed her.

"Are you hurt?" He whispered in her ear.

"I don't think so, no." Her whisper wasn't nearly as quiet, but that had more to do with the sheer panic that was building inside of her and needed a release.

Oh. My. God.

She had been shot at.

They had been shot at.

Yeah, the people she had worked with didn't have the safest job, but she had only been a listener of the dangerous missions. She recognized gunshots, but no one had ever fired a gun at her. This was not how she expected the evening to end.

On the brighter side of things, Danielle was fairly sure the alcohol had left her system and she wouldn't have to face the dreaded hangover Eleanor had alluded to.

"I saw both drop." A deep voice came from the general direction where the shots came from.

"That's not enough anymore. They want a visual confirmation and teeth as proof." A second voice responded.

"That's stupid. I saw them drop. Let's just get out of here."

"How'd that work out for the other teams, huh?" The second voice chastised.

While the men spoke, Leighton lifted his body slightly off of Danielle's. "Roll over. Quick."

She didn't need to be told twice. Once she was on her back, she looked up at Leighton's face, but he wasn't looking at her at all. His silver eyes were tracking something moving in the distance. Danielle resisted the urge to pat the top of his head and whisper good boy over and over. The wolf's appearance settled her nerves.

Everything about the situation was fucked up. She understood on some level that the Company would send someone out to eliminate her. Danielle had seen too much. They couldn't afford to let her exist outside of their control. But until the sound of that first shot, it had all been theoretical. Something that happened to other people.

Leighton shifted on top of her, then pressed his hand against hers. Was he comforting her? Reassuring her that everything would be okay?

Nope. He pressed something against her palm before he slipped off her and rolled out from under the branches of their makeshift shelter.

Her fingers wrapped around the warm object he pressed into her hand.

A handle.

A heavy handle.

Doing her best not to move enough to alert anyone of her hiding place, Danielle lifted her head to look down the length of her body. She didn't need to see what was in her hand, she could have guessed. But there were some times in life when things just had to be seen to be believed and what was happening right then was one of those times.

Yep. It was a knife. A double-edged knife that was really freaking long.

What was she going to do with a knife? Besides trip and stab herself with it. It didn't take more than a few seconds to find the answer.

Nothing.

Leighton didn't give her the knife to use unless everything went sideways, and she needed it. He expected her to stay hidden, and she planned on doing just that.

"Shit." It came from a voice that didn't belong to Leighton or any other pack member.

Danielle pushed away the urge to peek out from under the bush. The unknown was worse than knowing, but better than dying.

"I can't find them."

"Look for blood."

"Not seeing any."

"Fuck. Are you sure this is the right spot?"

"Cert–"

A gurgling and wheeze cut off the word. Then came a thump. Something heavy hit the ground.

"Shit." The second voice responded as Danielle thought the word.

The gurgle was easy to identify.

After years of listening in on missions, Danielle recognized the unique sound of a throat being slashed. From the second man's response, he must have known it too.

Danielle counted the seconds.

One thousand one.

One thousand two.

She'd make a run for the Lodge when she reached seven. It didn't matter if Danielle could find her way back or not, sitting still and hoping no one found her wouldn't end any better than getting lost in the woods with an assassin chasing after her.

One thousand three.

One thousand four.

"Fuckin' monster. It won't matter if you kill me. They'll just keep on sending teams until we've exterminated you." The gasping voice interrupted Danielle's counting.

Oh hell to the no.

She'd heard agents say similar things when they found themselves in situations with no escape. The words intended to incite and push away rational thought until the captor broke and killed the captured agent.

Potential scenarios flew through her mind, colliding with one another as she parsed her way through the data.

The assassin had more information. Something he was worried he might reveal under the right circumstances. But why didn't the company issue a suicide pill? If capture was a possibility, surely they would have given the men the means to kill themselves if there was even the slightest risk of revealing secrets. Unless the Company wasn't aware of the assassin's knowledge?

Oh shit, that was it. The Company might have sent the team out, but either the assassin or the team wasn't exclusive to the Company.

She had to stop Leighton from killing the assassin and all of her research told her that Leighton wouldn't be thinking clearly. He'd kill the assassin if it meant keeping his pack safe. Except in this case, killing the bastard wouldn't keep the pack safe and Danielle needed to stop Leighton.

She had spent all of her career with the Company protecting Vixen, keeping her safe from the idiots who used her skills to their advantage without caring how it affected her. Danielle wasn't willing to stop protecting Vixen just because she no longer worked for the Company.

Danielle rolled out from under the bush. Her hand gripped the hilt of the blade, as if she'd be able to use it with half the skill of Vixen. But unless the assassin had read Danielle's dossier, he wouldn't know that she was more likely to stab herself than a target.

"Leighton, No!" She spun around in a circle twice before her eyes found Leighton and the intruder in the shadow of an enormous tree.

Leighton's forearm pressed against the man's throat, cutting off his breath as he dangled several inches above the ground. No wonder his voice rasped when he spoke. The strength of Leighton's arm was enough to crush the man's esophagus.

Danielle shook the image from her mind. Thinking about the damage Leighton could do wasn't important. Stopping Leighton from committing that damage was the priority. To start, she needed to convince him to use the kinder choke-hold that was less likely to cause brain damage. They needed to be able to get coherent sentences from the man.

"Leighton?" Danielle raised her hands in the air, still holding the knife, and placed one foot in front of the other until she stood in front of both Leighton and the assassin. She stayed far enough away to remain out of reach of the assassin, but close enough for Leighton, and his wolf to see her.

Leighton's eyes flashed silver and held that bright glow. His wolf was close. Too close. One wrong move and the wolf would break free and maul the assassin. Not that the killer didn't deserve it, but they needed the man to stay alive long enough for Vixen to do her interrogation magic and pull the information out of him.

"Shift your arm, Leighton, so your elbow is in front of his throat."

Leighton and his wolf ignored her words. The man scratched at Leighton's forearm, but it didn't do any good. His feet twitched and his lips turned a pale blue.

Danielle pulled out the big gun. "Leighton, the others had to have heard the shots. They'll be here any minute and Vixen will want to question him. She can't question him if you've choked the air out of him."

Leighton's stare bored into her and it was all Danielle could do to keep from turning tail and running. His silver eyes spooked the hell out of her. The only thing keeping her in place was her certainty that, no matter what happened, Leighton's wolf would never hurt her. Or at least that's what she told herself because she rather liked the idea the wolf was smitten with her.

With a low growl that seemed to last for eternity, Leighton shifted his arm, using the polite choke-hold Danielle suggested. At the same time, claws pushed through the flesh on his fingers.

"Oh!" Danielle's eyes widened, "that's new."

Well, maybe not new to shifters, but from her limited amount of research she'd never heard of a shifter having an in between shift. Either they were the animal or the male. She'd have to remember to add that tidbit to her files.

The silver faded from Leighton's eyes as he rolled them at her declaration.

The man struggled against the new grasp, but Leighton's claws pressed against the flesh of his captive's neck. Danielle's eyes couldn't register much in the darkness, but she saw the dark red droplets of blood in the pale moon's light.

Leighton growled.

The man stilled.

Danielle lowered her arms and stepped backward. Right into a wall of muscle. Before she jumped and screamed, a firm hand wrapped around her bicep.

"Steady."

Bray. Bray was here. And if Bray was here, Vixen must be nearby.

"I'd love to say this is a surprise, but it isn't." Vixen stepped from the shadows and stood inches away from the man. Within a few seconds, she had his wrists shackled behind his back. "Leighton, you and Bray bring him to the shed and I'll meet you there."

Leighton didn't move. Instead, he stared at Danielle. Or maybe he stared at Bray. She couldn't tell.

Vixen stepped away from Leighton and followed his gaze to Danielle. "I'll bring her back to the Lodge. Once I'm sure she's safe, I'll meet you there. Okay?"

Bray cocked his head to the side, toward the general direction of the shed. "Jackson and Allard are taking care of the other body. The General, along with Finley and Tevin are watching Eleanor and Foster. There's no safer place than the Lodge and Vixen needs you."

The last sentence was enough to shake Leighton from whatever thoughts kept him frozen in place. He dropped the man, then grabbed him by his upper arm and dragged him away without looking back at Danielle even once.

She tried to hide her disappointment. Whatever she had been expecting, it wasn't Leighton ignoring her as he dragged the prisoner away with Bray's help.

Vixen took a deep breath from Danielle's side.

"Sheesh," Danielle jumped and pressed her hand against her chest, as though it would slow her racing heart. "You all just appear out of nowhere. How do you do that?"

"Practice." Vixen grinned at Danielle and winked. "Come on, before Leighton loses his shit when I don't show up quick enough. The last thing we need is his wolf on a protective streak. The animal doesn't do well differentiating friend from foe when he's keeping someone safe."

"Friend or foe?" Danielle hurried to keep pace with Vixen.

"Yep. And from what I've seen, both Leighton and his wolf will do anything to keep you safe." Vixen looked down at Danielle's hand. "That knife? I gave it to him. Leighton doesn't let anyone touch it. Not even me."

Danielle raised her hand and looked at the knife. "Do you want it back?"

"Nope. Watch your step."

"Oh." Danielle looked down in time to stop herself from tripping over a root. She lowered her hand and made certain the blade pointed down. Safety first, right? "Are you sure you don't want the knife?"

"Leighton gave it to you. If you give it away his wolf will take offense and blame him. That's the last thing Leighton needs right now."

Vixen stopped walking and Danielle almost bumped into her. "Um..."

"The General's on the porch waiting for you." Vixen nodded to the large house built into the mountain. "You might feel more sober with the rush of adrenaline from our guest's surprise visit. You aren't. The General is going to talk to you about a task. You'll want to get started on it right away. Don't. Go to bed and get some sleep. You can start it in the morning after your body's metabolized all the alcohol."

Danielle looked to her right, expecting to find Vixen still there, but she was gone.

"Hurry, Ms. Howe. Roose and Mac are waiting for you to get inside before they head out to patrol the forest." The General called to her from the porch.

She closed her eyes and counted to three before walking the rest of the way across the yard to the house. Or lodge. Or whatever the hell they called it. Danielle already had enough information she needed to process and wasn't sure she wanted to add more.

Maybe she could convince the General to hold off until the morning before he set her on whatever task he and Vixen had dreamed up?

CHAPTER ELEVEN

AS SOON as Danielle made it to the porch, the General yanked her inside. He closed and locked the door before sending her down to her bedroom and away from the windows. She didn't even have time to ask about the task Vixen mentioned before he resumed guarding the door and checking in on the others through two-way radios. She made a mental note to find a better communication protocol.

Eleanor waited for Danielle outside her room and walked in behind her without an invitation.

"Do you want to try to sleep?" Eleanor sat down on the bed.

Danielle shook her head, "I'll wait for the others to come back."

"Yeah, I guessed as much. If you don't mind, I'll wait with you."

"What about Foster? Don't you want to be with him?"

Eleanor snorted. "Right now Uncle Finley is keeping Foster's wolf distracted and entertained. He's been through this drill a few times and for him it's one big game."

Pulling her knees up to her chest and wrapping her arms around her legs, Danielle stared at Hampstead running on his wheel. "He picked up my hamster for me."

"Yeah, about that..." Eleanor looked over her shoulder at the fluffy rodent.

Danielle glanced away from Hampstead and looked at Eleanor. "About what?"

"I'm apologizing now. We're doing our best to keep Foster away, but he will find a way into your room at some point and he will find a way to let the hamster out."

Eleanor sounded so distraught, Danielle wasn't sure whether to comfort her new friend or laugh. "Hampstead is an escape artist. He'll find a way out of his cage before Foster figures out how to get into my room and open the cage."

"Err." Eleanor bit down on her thumb. "Have you considered what will happen to a hamster free from his cage with a wolf pack? The wolves hunt. I haven't seen them go after mice, but then I don't look too closely at what they hunt. And Foster is in the middle of a frog phase. Thank God the weather has cooled down enough for the frogs to go underground."

Danielle laughed. "That bad?"

"The legs twitch as his pup swallows it down. And then it comes right back up if he shifts back too soon. Bray and Jackson keep telling me he'll learn soon enough, but I think they're just lying to comfort me."

"Maybe I should find a better place for Hampstead."

"You can't. Trust me on this, Leighton will get upset."

"That's the second time I've heard that tonight." Danielle stretched her legs out and leaned back on the bed.

"Leighton has always kept his distance. He takes part in pack stuff, but stays on the outskirts unless Vixen forces him to get involved. He can't say no to her."

"Okay?"

"Well, he's always held himself apart until you. This is huge for Leighton and I think we're all worried what might happen if his wolf thinks you're rejecting him."

"His wolf would never hurt me. Don't ask me how I know this, but I do."

"It's not you we're worried about. His wolf will punish him. Or at least that's my theory. Vixen won't comment whenever I bring it up, but since she isn't denying it, I figure I have to be close to the truth." The front door slammed and Eleanor jerked at the sound. "They're back."

Danielle stared at the closed door to her bedroom. "That was fast."

"Vixen is efficient."

Danielle nodded in agreement.

"They'll have a pack meeting. Roose and Mac will be there too."

"Oh." Danielle wasn't sure if Eleanor needed to leave for the meeting. "You should probably go see Jackson."

"You don't get out of it that easily." Eleanor jumped off the bed and reached for Danielle's hand. "You're in this pack too now."

Danielle allowed herself to be pulled from the bed, but grabbed the glass of water before Eleanor dragged her out the door. "You sure about this?"

"Yep. I mean, unless you'd rather stay here?" Eleanor winked at Danielle as she opened the door.

Danielle had the decency to blush. There was no way she'd want to stay in her room when everyone else was talking and she would have found a way to listen in on the meeting.

Eleanor stopped in front of a closed door and knocked.

Finley cracked the door open and peeked his head out. "I'll be there as soon as he falls asleep."

"Want me to put him to bed so you can go to the meeting?" Eleanor asked.

"Nah, he's close to crashing. Between the barbecue and the excitement, I doubt he'll be able to stay awake much longer. I'll be there in a bit." Finley grinned at Eleanor. "Besides, if you don't go, Jackson will come down then Vixen will get impatient and Bray will get frustrated and the meeting will blow up."

"You know everyone so well, Finley." Eleanor returned his grin. "Thanks for getting him to bed."

"Anytime." Finley closed the door, leaving Eleanor and Danielle standing alone in the empty hallway.

"There you two are." Mac turned down the hallway and headed toward the two women. "I was just on my way to get you. Vixen is waiting for everyone before starting."

As soon as they walked into the sizable living area, Mac headed to Vixen, Bray, and the General and Eleanor made a beeline toward Jackson, who scooped her up and pulled her close to his chest. Danielle watched it all happen and never felt more out of place in her life. She didn't belong to anyone and the one she wanted to belong to couldn't seem to decide what he or his wolf wanted.

She glanced around the room with as much nonchalance as she could muster, considering the situation, until her gaze landed on Leighton. As if he sensed her attention, he lifted his broody stare from the floor and leveled it on her. His eyes flashed silver before returning to their steady blue. Other than the glimpse of his wolf, Leighton didn't show anything else. None of the worry of Jackson and Bray, or the wary expressions on the others' faces.

The male was like a boulder that had come to life. Except a boulder would have shown more emotion.

Danielle looked away. After their conversation, she had hoped he wouldn't close down behind the giant walls of defense he'd built up over the years. Granted her words had been well-lubricated with the amount of alcohol in her system and the conversation might not have gone exactly as she remembered, but she had thought they had made a breakthrough before the whole shooting fiasco started.

Leighton's arms dropped to his side, and he walked away from Roose and Tevin without a word. The others continued their conversation as if Leighton hadn't been there to begin with, and Danielle assumed he walked away mid conversation a lot, but they were used to it.

Except Leighton wasn't walking away from them. He was walking towards her. Well, more striding than walking. He crossed the entire room in less than six long steps when it would have taken Danielle at least twenty.

She sighed in relief. He didn't look hurt. She had been worried since she left him that the assassin would do something stupid and cause harm to Leighton. Dried blood decorated his shirt and jeans, but it wasn't his. She didn't understand how she knew, but something she was willing to listen to told her it wasn't his.

As soon as she was within reach, Leighton wrapped his arms around her and pulled her close to him. Lifting her off the ground, he pressed his mouth to the top of her head and took a deep breath. A low growl rumbled from his chest causing her body to vibrate.

"Are you hurt?" Leighton asked.

"I'm fine, Leighton. A little shaken, but fine." She wriggled in his arms and tilted her head back. "You protected me and kept me safe."

"My wolf and I smelled your fear. We needed to make sure nothing happened to you. That you weren't hurt."

"You did that, Leighton. You and your wolf did that."

Leighton lifted his head enough for her to look in his eyes. "I didn't want to leave, but we needed to keep you safe."

"I know." She didn't know. Not really, but Leighton didn't need her confusion at that moment. He needed her unconditional understanding. "You kept me safe."

"What if I wasn't there? What if I let you run off?"

"But you didn't."

"You aren't safe here, Dani, but you aren't safe anywhere else, are you?"

"I don't think so." Danielle shook her head.

"How bad is it? Vixen sent us out of the shed when she began her interrogation."

Of course she would. The Pack had likely never witnessed Vixen in pure sociopath mode where she was capable of inflicting excruciating pain and suffering to get the answers she needed. Danielle had never seen it herself, but she had heard recordings. The sounds had been bad enough. She didn't want to think about the accompanying visuals.

"I'm not sure, but assuming the Company ramps up their missions, it's worse than you think. When the man said they'd send another team, he wasn't wrong. The only advantage you have right now is Vixen. She's always been their secret weapon, their last resort. Her replacement hasn't been named. Probably hasn't even been trained yet."

Realization hit her as soon as the words left her mouth. She looked over Leighton's shoulder at Vixen.

The legend of Unit D stared back for a few moments before lowering her eyes. Vixen figured it out too. She'd likely known since Danielle broke the coded orders to bring Foster in alive. The Company wanted another shifter in Unit D, but one they could condition from a young age. Danielle wanted to vomit and hoped Eleanor never learned the truth.

Leighton buried his face in her neck and took another deep breath before setting Danielle back down on her feet.

The front door opened and everyone in the room turned toward it. Jackson pushed Eleanor behind him and Leighton stepped in front of Danielle, blocking her view with his massive body.

"Computer girl?" Allard called out as he walked into the room.

Figuring he must be talking to her, Danielle peeked around Leighton's shoulder. "Yeah?"

Allard raised his arm and waved a satellite phone at her. "The guy Leighton dropped in the woods had this on him. Figured you'd want it?"

Leighton's arm shot out to catch the phone Allard tossed her way

"Battery?" Danielle asked.

"Removed." The battery followed the phone's trajectory and once more, Leighton caught it.

"Everything taken care of?" Vixen asked.

"All cleaned up." Allard nodded.

"Once Finley gets here, we'll get started."

As if Vixen's announcement was a cue for a well-choreographed maneuver, everyone in the room found a seat. There wasn't the usual shuffling about trying to find a free chair or even the pushing and shoving Danielle remembered from the few meetings she had attended while at the Company. She looked around the room for a free seat, but Leighton pulled her down onto the cushion next to him and wrapped his arm around her shoulder.

Danielle slipped the phone and battery from Leighton's hand and leaned into the warm space under Leighton's arm. She replaced the battery and turned on the phone. As soon as the screen flickered to life, she pressed a code into the number pad. It didn't make the phone invincible to listening in attempts, but the code made it more difficult. For a moment she worried the code wouldn't be accepted, but the phone flashed its acknowledgment of her order.

"Stupid."

"Hmm?" Leighton bent his neck forward and kissed the top of Danielle's head.

She ignored the gesture. "Whoever is running these teams didn't change out the tech. I set them up, including putting in protections so they can't be used against us. If I was still there, I would have replaced everything with a microchip."

"I know once you get started on a project, we won't be able to pull you away from it. Plus, I doubt there's anything worthwhile on there." Vixen leveled her gaze on the phone in Danielle's hand. "Mind waiting until we're done? Then you can spend all night locked away in your room tearing into it.

Vixen wasn't wrong. The phone would turn into a distraction. Even if Danielle couldn't find anything, she wouldn't give up until she had exhausted every nook and cranny that might hide a secret that would help the pack. Especially after figuring out the Company's attraction to Foster

CHAPTER TWELVE

"**YOU** did good. When we were in the woods, you did really good." Leighton pressed his lips against Danielle's ear and whispered.

Danielle blushed. She'd never handled compliments well, and hearing one from Leighton felt weird, as though she didn't deserve it. And she didn't, really. All Danielle did was hide under a bush while Leighton did all the heavy lifting.

"Foster's asleep, but it's anyone's guess for how long." Finley sauntered into the room and flopped down on a large armchair.

"You're like the Foster whisperer, Finley. I don't know what your secret is, but you need to bottle it up and sell it. Moms and dads would buy it up by the caseload."

"If we're all done coming up with a fictional product that would never meet FDA standards?" When no one responded, Vixen smirked. "All right then, Let's get started. We're going back to nightly patrols.

Gareth volunteered the members of his pride. They'd be here now if they weren't taking tonight's patrol."

Danielle flipped open the Rolodex in her mind and scanned through all the names associated with Broken Peak Pack and their friends. Gareth wasn't anywhere. She hadn't seen the name or heard any mention of it in passing.

"Gareth is a friend, but even more off the grid than this group. Without him, Eleanor and Foster would never have found Broken Peak. Wayne Ritchie and Gareth are cousins." The General read the confusion on Danielle's face. "No one associated with Unit D or the government has heard about Gareth because he and his pride are ghosts. They might as well be NOC agents in the Company. Hell, it wouldn't surprise me if Gareth was a NOC."

"He wasn't." Vixen was certain in her declaration.

Both the General and Danielle raised an eyebrow, but didn't question Vixen's knowledge.

"Along with the nightly patrols, no one steps off the porch alone. Bray and I are instituting a buddy system. Unit D went rogue and is serving two masters. The Company isn't issuing the salted earth orders, that's coming from a higher power."

"Higher power?" Jackson asked.

Vixen just nodded.

Danielle swallowed hard. There was only one higher power than the Company. If Vixen went after him, war would break out between the shifters and the country.

"If they haven't changed the tech, I can use it against them." Danielle changed the subject to the phone in her hand before anyone else figured it out. "All my tech has a signature. I could set up a net. A few receivers in the right place and as soon as the tech crossed that invisible border, an alarm would go off. You'd know they were here before they got close enough to do any damage. Eventually they'll figure it out. Or I hope they do, because if they don't it means whoever took over my job is a certified moron."

Tevin and Allard stopped fighting over the small couch with their man-spreading long enough to look up at Danielle with goofy grins.

"I like her," Tevin stated.

"Can we keep her?" Allard asked.

"No one's keeping her. This pack isn't safe for anyone, especially a human." Leighton growled.

Danielle flinched away, and Leighton didn't stop her. After everything he'd said before, she shouldn't have expected anything different from him. She wanted to run away, to leave the pack to their little meeting and hide under her bed. Or maybe she could find where they secreted away her Volvo P1800 and drive off into the proverbial sunset, leaving Leighton behind in the proverbial dust.

Before she said what she wanted to say, which was to call Leighton a number of names (most of which included the word douche), she breathed out through her nose and narrowed her eyes at the General. After all, it was his fault for bringing her here. "Can we get on with this so I can get the system set up? The faster I get it up, the longer you can use it before someone smart enough comes in and replaces the tech."

Leighton shot up from the couch and stomped down the hallway toward the kitchen.

"Well, fuck." Finley slumped down in his seat.

"Yep, that's a definite fuck." Eleanor agreed as she watched Leighton's retreat.

Bray pushed to his feet and padded across the room. Leaning against the wall of the hallway, he crossed his arms over his chest and studied Leighton's back. "Did anyone check him over for injuries?"

"Bray..." Vixen stopped his chastisements.

He looked over his shoulder at his mate. "Not criticizing, Vi, I didn't bother asking if he was hurt either." He turned his steady stare down the hallway and called down to Leighton. "Go wash up, and then we'll meet in the kitchen. Our discussion's not over, but it will take forever if we don't get some meat in you."

Leighton didn't respond, at least not that Danielle heard. Maybe the shifters couldn't just read minds, what if they could communicate with each other in their thoughts? Nah. Danielle pushed that idea away as fast as it arrived. Any silent communication they shared probably came from their animals. Which eliminated humans from the equation.

"I saw that." Bray growled out in a low tone.

"Good. You were supposed to." Leighton bellowed back.

"Shh," Eleanor narrowed her eyes and tapped her foot against the old braided rug on the hardwood floor. "If any of you idiots wake Foster, you can be the one to get up with him before the crack of dawn and deal with his grumpy furry butt."

The room crackled with an electric charge that stood the hair on Danielle's arms up on end.

"Vi!" Bray snapped.

"What?" Vixen jerked back and raised her hands up.

"Bring it back under control," Mac spoke in the same tones some-one used with a panicked animal. "Your griffin is doing that accidental power seepage thing again."

As Danielle looked around the room, everyone looked at either Bray or Vixen with their chins lifted and their eyes down. She never felt more out of place. Leighton was right. She didn't belong at Broken Peak.

Eleanor elbowed Jackson in the ribs. "Come on, let's get food ready. I think I have some chili in the freezer we can heat up."

As the pair headed out of the common room and toward the kitchen, the others skirted around Vixen and Bray before following Eleanor and

Jackson to the kitchen. Roose trailed behind the others, not wanting to stay around either. The General and Mac were the only two left in the room besides Danielle and the last place she wanted to be was between Bray and Vixen when Vixen was having an accidental power seepage situation, whatever that meant.

Danielle hopped to her feet and scurried after the others. Except, instead of heading to the kitchen, she turned down the hallway to the bedrooms. Even if she hadn't known which room was Leighton's, she'd be able to tell by the sound of the door slamming against the wall.

It would be a complete miracle if Foster slept through Leighton's stomping and slamming and clomping about. Danielle didn't doubt for a minute that Eleanor would follow through on her threat and send the pup to Leighton when Foster woke up at the crack of dawn.

Danielle followed Leighton into his room. The little voice living inside her head who liked to point out poor decisions screamed out all the reasons why it wasn't the best idea to enter his room and pointed out why she should head back to the kitchen with the others. She ignored that voice.

In for a penny, in for a pound. Right?

Leighton stood in front of the dresser, with his hands pressed against the top and his head bowed. He didn't look at her, but he knew she was there. His body stiffened when Danielle walked in.

At least he hadn't told her to get out.

Yet.

Danielle closed the door and leaned against it, watching Leighton in silence.

His fingers dug into the wood, and he rumbled out a roar.

"You'll wake Foster."

"Nothing's right. It's all wrong."

"Leighton..." She wasn't sure what to say.

For the first time since she met him, Danielle saw something in him she hadn't seen before. His feelings on full display. Every time she watched him with the pack, Leighton kept a tight rein on his emotions. The male standing across the room from her wasn't the same male she observed since arriving at Broken Peak.

"I just don't know."

Danielle released a long breath. "A lot of things got talked about tonight, Leighton. I don't know which topic not knowing applies to."

"You. Me. Everything." Leighton pushed away from his dresser and collapsed on his bed. Resting his elbows on his knees, he stared down at his thumbs. "It was easier when I didn't have to worry about not knowing."

She sat next to him and crossed one leg over the other while flexing her foot, admiring her Uggs. "When I first joined the Company, they told me not to get invested in the agents or their assets. Assets are expendable. Or at least they are under everyone but Vixen. But here's the problem with not getting invested, you stop caring, because when you care, you inevitably get hurt. Not worrying about not knowing is the same thing as not getting invested and not caring. I took my cues from Vixen before I even knew who she was. Maybe you should too?"

"I talk to her."

"About this?"

Leighton lifted his head long enough to glare at her.

"Your desire to not have to worry about not knowing, which I think means you don't want to care, doesn't seem like it's going to happen."

Leighton added a growl to his glare.

"You have three options here: accept that you care and will get hurt at some point because that's one of the side effects of caring, ignore that you care and still get hurt at some point, or convince yourself that you don't care, but again, you'll still get hurt." Danielle counted the options off on her fingers. "I get it, you don't want to care, but I'm not sure that's possible."

"It's not that."

"Then what is it?" Danielle spread her arms out with her palms up and threw her head back to stare at the ceiling. As if the small cobweb stuck to the exposed beam could answer the question for her.

"I care. I care for Foster and Bray and Vixen. I care for the pack. And I care for you. But Broken Peak isn't a sanctuary anymore. It's not safe. And if I can't convince you to leave and I can't keep you safe, then what happened tonight is going to seem like paradise. If you stay here, I can't promise I'll be able to protect you."

"So, let me get this right. Despite Vixen and the General thinking this is the safest place for me at the moment, you don't agree with them and you want me to hate you enough that I'll leave even if Vixen and the General have said they won't let me leave?"

"That's not it either."

Danielle jumped to her feet and paced in front of Leighton. "Then explain it to me, because I'm all out of theories. And that doesn't happen often for me."

"Me, Dani. I can't keep you safe from me. You're it for me. You're the one my wolf chose and I can't do anything about it. The longer you stay, the harder it will be for my wolf and me when you leave."

She stopped her pacing and spun on her heel to face him. "What?"

Yeah, what was a stupid thing to say. She knew it as soon as it came out of her mouth, but she couldn't do anything once it was out in the wild. It would have been nice to have a delete button in life, but until someone came up with one, she was stuck with regretting the stupid things she said for a few seconds before moving past them.

Leighton buried his face in his hands and spoke into his palms. "Dani, my father wasn't a good mate or a male."

"You said that already. You know, before the whole getting shot at thing happened."

"He and his wolf claimed my mother even though she didn't want to mate my father. He claimed her by force."

Danielle could have walked away then. She could have left Leighton's room and done her best to ignore him for the rest of her time at Broken Peak, for however long that would be. But she didn't.

Once again she told that silly voice in her head who liked to give her advice to shut the hell up. And before that silly voice came up with reasonable excuses why she shouldn't do what she was about to do, Danielle stalked toward Leighton, wrapped her hands around his wrists and tugged his hands away from his face. She crawled onto his lap with her knees pressed against the outside of his legs as she straddled his thighs. "You aren't your father, Leighton, and I'm going to keep telling you that until it sinks in."

Leighton's eyes silvered as both he and his wolf studied Danielle's face, looking for an answer to an unasked question.

Eventually he found the answer he was looking for. Or maybe he didn't, but decided it didn't matter. Danielle didn't care much either way.

Leighton twisted his wrists free from her grip. Instead of pulling away, he placed his hands on her waist and stroked up her sides to her ribs before returning his hands to her waist. A shiver ran through her body at his touch.

"I'm not good at this either, you know? I don't have any role models who showed me how to be good at this. The longest relationship I've had with anyone other than my grandma is my hamster and every other relationship is predicated on the other party knowing me by a code name." She pressed her hands against his cheeks and tilted his head back so he was looking at her. Sometimes it wasn't just easier to change the subject, it was better. This was one of those times. "Bray asked if anyone had checked on you. What did he mean?"

Leighton brought his thick fingers to the buttons of his shirt. He didn't turn his head away, but he lowered his gaze as he unbuttoned the flannel. When he pulled the shirt open, a full array of dark blue and purple bruises decorated his chest. From the way the bruises spread and stretched across his skin, they looked as though they wrapped around his sides to his back.

Despite Danielle's best intentions to keep her reactions to herself, a tiny gasp escaped. Her fingertips hovered over his skin, not wanting to touch his bruises and cause him more hurt. "Oh, Leighton..."

He shrugged and her fingers accidentally brushed his skin, but he didn't flinch away from her touch, even though it likely caused him a lot of discomfort. "Once I eat something, they'll fade. At the time, I didn't care what happened to me as long as you were safe. I had to take a bit of a beating to keep him from getting close to your hiding place."

There were a lot of things Danielle could do or say at that moment, but she opted for the inappropriate. She leaned back and dropped her cardigan down her arms to the floor. The tank top slipped forward and gave Leighton a delightful view of her cleavage.

The heavy fabric of her khakis rubbed against the heavy denim of Leighton's jeans. For the briefest of moments, she wished she had worn one of her dresses. Two layers of heavy fabric, not including any underwear, was two too many as far as Danielle was concerned. She bent forward, keeping her fingers clear of his bruises. She pressed her lips against his, then pulled his bottom lip between her teeth.

Leighton growled, his hands slid down to her hips, and her fingers pressed into the soft flesh of her ass. His hips lifted, grinding against her as he pulled her down at the same time. It was impossible to mistake the thick shaft pressing up against her as a gun in his pocket. Leighton was definitely happy to see her, or at least a certain part of his body was.

She yanked her hands back before pressing them against his chest. The last thing she wanted was to pull him out of whatever was happening by causing him more pain and reminding him of his injuries. She settled for resting her palms on his shoulders.

He chuckled at her hesitation before pulling his lip from her teeth. Leighton groaned, "Dani..."

Her mouth chased after his lips, "hmm?"

"You're gonna kill my self-control."

"And that's bad, why?"

She didn't give up pursuit of his mouth, but Leighton seemed to have more fun playing keep away from her than answering her question.

Danielle let out a whimper as the frustration built up inside her. She'd never wanted something so badly in her life. "Leighton."

He rolled his hips against her and caught her mouth with his. His tongue delved between her lips and dove into her mouth. A tiny growl came from Danielle and Leighton tilted his head to the side to deepen the kiss. Apparently, he enjoyed her impersonation of a wolf. She filed that information away for later.

Leighton yanked her hips forward and brushed his thumbs along the front of her hip bones as he moved them closer to her clit. Once his thumbs reached their goal, he used one thumb to stretch her flesh so her clit poked out, rubbing against the soft fabric of her panties. It shouldn't have felt as good as it did.

But that also might have more to do with the fluttering of nervous energy manifesting itself as butterfly wings tickling their way down from her belly to the source of pleasure Leighton was giving her. If she considered that not only would Leighton be able to tell she was aroused from her damp panties, but that he could also smell her arousal in the air, Danielle would have blushed.

"Leighton, please." She dragged out the word please and wiggled on his lap, wanting more from him.

Her eyes widened. Granted things always seemed bigger when you couldn't see them, but the massive object currently pressing against her and growing even larger, was enormous. Even by porn and novelty store items for bachelorette parties standards, it was huge.

Danielle was done waiting. She was done letting Leighton lead them along. She fantasized about this too many times to not have it play out, even if she had to make that happen herself. Breaking from their kiss, she slipped off his lap. In an uncoordinated and graceless maneuver, she pulled off her pants and boots at the same time then crawled back onto his lap and went back to kissing him. She even reached down and returned his hands to her hips.

There was no way he'd be able to ignore the blatant signals she was sending his way.

Her hands made their way back to his shoulders, gently dancing over his bruised flesh, but Leighton didn't flinch away from her touch.

"Please," she whimpered out her plea between kisses.

"Please what?" Leighton growled, sending ripples of even more pleasure through her.

"Please make me come, Leighton."

"Is that what you want, Dani? For me to make you come on my hand?" His thumb circled her clit and his fingers pressed against the silky material of her panties.

"I don't care how I come, as long as I do."

Where were these words coming from? Danielle had always been quiet during sex. But here, with Leighton, she lost the filter that prevented her from saying the dirty words she was thinking.

"Is this what you want?" Leighton slipped a thick finger under her panties and inside of her.

"Yesss," she hissed out. Her fingers bit into his shoulders and her head fell back as he slid a second finger into her.

Holy crap. His fingers were huge and not even half the size of the monster cock hiding in his jeans. If his fingers stretched her apart, what would his dick feel like inside of her?

His thumb pressed down hard on her clit and she gave up whatever pretense of control she thought she had. Danielle bounced up and down on his hand, riding him faster and harder as he drew her pleasure closer and closer to the brink.

So close. She was close, but it wasn't going to be enough.

She lifted off his lap and reached between them only to fumble her way through unbuttoning his jeans and pulling his hard dick free.

Leighton growled once. His hand, still on her hip, bit into her flesh while his other hand, still working on giving her pleasure, ripped her panties right off.

She'd have bruises in the morning from his hand on her hips and a mark from the ripped off panties, but she didn't care. She needed him inside her. Wrapping her hand around the base of his cock, she guided him to her entrance. Her thighs trembled from the effort of keeping herself from being impaled on his hard dick. She lowered herself down, giving her body time to adjust to the thick shaft.

Remembering the noise Leighton made earlier, Danielle nipped at his bottom lip and nibbled her way down his neck to the taut trapezoid muscle. Something inside her convinced her to bite down on the muscle. As soon as her teeth pressed into his flesh, Leighton growled out a roar and thrust up hard while pulling down on her hips at the same time.

Their hips rocked together in time and Leighton lost whatever grip he had on his control. He stood up, keeping his cock deep inside her and turned so he faced the bed. Lowering her down on the soft mattress, Leighton followed her body, maintaining his long hard thrusts.

Danielle bit down harder on his muscle and his cock jerked inside her.

"Dani," Leighton growled, "I'm close. So close. Make yourself come for me."

She didn't need to reach down between them and help herself along. Leighton hit all the right spots until the pleasure overflowed. His fingers drew her to the edge, but his hard cock pushed her right over.

Her orgasm hit, and she shattered around him. The world shook. And she exploded again.

All the cliches and metaphors for great sex and earth moving orgasms hit her at once. Danielle had thought they only existed in Romance novels and her fantasies of Leighton. But her fantasies weren't far from the truth.

"Bite me," Leighton groaned through gritted teeth.

She obliged his request and bit down hard in the same spot. She must have broken his skin because a hint of iron hit her tongue. The thought left her brain as soon as it entered when Leighton rammed into her hard enough to push her across the bed. His cock jerked with his release and her body tightened around him as he pulled another orgasm from her.

With a groan Leighton pulled out of her, but not away. He wrapped his arms around her, moved with her until their heads rested on the pillows and their feet pointed to the foot of the bed.

"Leighton?"

"Give me ten minutes, woman. Ten minutes with you in my arms and my wolf content and then I'll do whatever you want."

CHAPTER THIRTEEN

DANI was still sound asleep when Leighton woke up just before the sun rose. His wolf woke him, wanting the chance to run through the quiet forest before the day's chaos arrived. And both man and wolf were in complete agreement.

For the first night in a long time Leighton slept soundly and didn't wake up in the morning still half asleep. No nightmares or even bad dreams marred his sleep. Nights passed without nightmares before, but a night had never passed without bad dreams.

Leighton pressed a kiss to her forehead then slipped out of bed, careful not to wake Dani. He grabbed his pair of jeans from the floor and pulled them on before heading through the quiet house. The sun hadn't risen yet, which explained why no one else was up. Except for Gareth's mountain lions out on patrol, the woods should be empty. Leighton's wolf was thrilled with the prospect. He loved wandering alone through the forest without the chance of running into any packmates more than he loved shredding Leighton from the inside.

Instead of dropping his jeans and letting his wolf out, he walked across the yard and headed into the woods. The peace of the quiet woods put the male at ease too. Leighton had a lot on his mind. Between what Dani and his wolf were telling him, Leighton had to rethink the whole not taking a mate idea. The wolf voted already. He voted the first time he saw Dani with an enthusiastic yes. Leighton wasn't completely convinced it was the best decision.

What if he did something stupid and hurt her? No, not if, when. When he did something stupid and hurt her.

Leighton's wolf perked up and pushed closer to the surface, but not because he wanted to run. Someone was approaching. Since his wolf wasn't on edge, he assumed friend and not foe. He lifted his chin and sniffed at the air. Vixen. She must have followed him out.

Vixen fell into step next to Leighton before he could shift and race off. Not that avoiding Vixen ever worked. The female had a tenacity that sometimes even surprised Bray.

"She's your mate, right?"

"Probably." Leighton didn't bother with denials as he stepped over a fallen branch. "How d'you guess?"

"There's a long list, but the clincher was last night. No night-mares. With everything that happened, I expected them in full force."

"She's only been here a few days, how long a list could it be?"

"You picked up her hamster. Just high-tailed it to the city, faced punishment from Bray, and me too, for racing off, and didn't bother to call and tell us what was going on until you were on your way back. And last night, before the shit hit the fan, you glared at anyone who so much as looked at Danielle for more than a few seconds. Bray and I had our suspicions, but not having any nightmares last night, that's when we knew for sure."

"How come you never forced me to tell you about the nightmares?"

"Would it have helped if I had?"

He considered the question, but didn't have a satisfactory answer for her.

Vixen stopped in front of a large tree, one with low branches that her griffin enjoyed perching on. "Better yet, ask yourself whether you'd answer me honestly?"

Leighton leaned against a smaller tree close to the one Vixen stood by and shook his head. "No, probably not."

"So why bother?"

Some people tried to pull out answers no matter the cost, but not Vixen. She didn't beat around the bush or make any of the pack talk about their feelings. Not that Leighton and his packmates discussed their feelings on a regular basis. It was pretty much only Jackson who talked about feelings and only when Eleanor forced it.

Maybe it was time to discuss things. That's what mates were supposed to do, right? Even though Vixen wasn't his mate, it might be good practice for when Dani would inevitably want to talk about the feelings thing.

"I can't save anyone."

"Those are the worst. Just when you think you have the perfect plan in place, everything changes."

He hadn't expected her to understand, but that was less a commentary about Vixen and more a commentary about Leighton's expectations of others. He took the plunge and shared some of the dreams that haunted his sleep. "Before you came, father showed up and attacked my pack while I stood around helpless."

"And after I came?"

"It was the men who attacked you. And I couldn't save you. Then Eleanor and Foster showed up and no matter what I did, Foster always died."

"Just because you didn't have any nightmares last night doesn't mean they're gone for good. There are some nights when mine revisit, even with Bray there."

"I know." And he did. Though it surprised him that Dani witnessing his nightmares didn't bother him.

"Shit happens to us, Leighton, and our minds are usually good at keeping us safe. But every so often our brains utterly fail. I'd like to say that things get better, but that's not true. We just get better at dealing with them."

Leighton laughed. He shouldn't have though. Their conversation was a serious one, and Vixen hadn't cracked a smile once since she joined him. But her blunt and honest advice chased away any concerns he didn't realize he had, and he felt lighter.

Vixen gave him an approximation of a shrug and the right corner of her mouth lifted in a way that some people might consider a grin if they closed one eye and tilted their head to the side. On the scale of Vixen approvals rating, the gesture landed somewhere around five or six.

"Is that why you're out here with me now? You wanted to ask about my nightmares."

"Oh God, no. I figured you'd talk about them when you were ready. This is more of the talk about your intentions with Danielle. The General noticed your attraction to her last night and wanted to talk with you since her parents aren't in the picture. He's kind of old-fashioned that way. I didn't think you wanted to have this conversation with him, so I volunteered."

"General Jesup wanted to intimidate me?"

"He's protective of Danielle. And for good reason. She's put herself in the cross hairs of some dangerous people. I didn't share this with the pack, Leighton, but the General insisted he bring her here. He said this was the only place she'd be safe."

"I thought it was your idea. Bray told us it was your idea. You didn't tell Bray the General insisted?"

Vixen rolled her eyes. "Please. Bray's paranoid enough for the both of us. If he knew it was all the General's idea, Bray would think Danielle was a mole. Which she isn't. Bray and I share a lot of things, most everything. But sometimes, there are times when we keep things from each other because knowing about them wouldn't change the outcome. He keeps things from me too. Eventually we learn the truth, but as long as it's not about us as an us, we trust each other to do what's best. Whether Danielle coming here was my idea or the General's doesn't matter. She'd be here, regardless. Plus, the way this pack has been working, she'd stumble into the territory for some odd reason or another that had nothing to do with me or the work she did for the Company."

Every so often Vixen had a way of sharing advice without it sounding like advice. The hard part was figuring out when she was doing it. Leighton experienced it enough when he trained with her that he didn't miss her message. It's okay to keep some things from Dani, but he better be prepared to share the stuff that matters.

"So. What are your intentions?"

"Simple. She's my mate, and I plan on making it official as long as she agrees." Leighton didn't hesitate. He wanted her the first time he saw her, he just hadn't come to terms with it yet. Dani had done that. Pushed him to face his feelings.

"Have you talked to her about it yet? She doesn't have the benefit of a voice living inside her head advising her. Danielle might have an idea about shifters and mates, but it's all in the abstract."

Had he? Dani and Leighton had talked about a lot of things, but he'd been so frightened of the idea of not being able to keep her safe that he hadn't told her what he wanted. He'd have to change that. Dani deserved to know exactly how he felt and not just how his wolf felt.

"And once more back to the feelings."

"What?"

Leighton hadn't realized he said the words instead of thinking them. "Nothing. Just that feelings seem to happen a lot more since Dani showed up."

Vixen grinned one of her *the jokes on you* smiles. "Yeah. Mates tend to do that. If it makes the mental gymnastics you're enduring any better, I wasn't ready to face mine until the night Bray woke my griffin."

They hadn't talked about the night Vixen nearly died and Bray brought her back by claiming her. Instead, the pack talked around the subject. Even Mac avoided talking to her about it. She talked to Eleanor about it, but Leighton only knew that because he walked in on them once when Eleanor was interviewing Vixen. Something about research and figuring out if there might be other griffins in the world Mac didn't know about.

God help them all if there were more griffins.

"I didn't realize what Bray was to me until it was almost too late. It was too late, but Bray changed fate that night." Vixen looked up at the sky, then headed back to the Lodge. "Don't wait until it's too late, Leighton. Tell her how you feel. She's a smart girl and is good at calculating risks. You're the last thing you need to protect her from."

She left Leighton behind with his thoughts. That was the second time he heard Dani could protect herself. Maybe it was time to listen to it.

He took the long way back to the lodge, walking around the perimeter of the tree line. With each step he composed the words he'd say to her. His wolf wasn't any help. All he wanted to do was claim her. In fact, the wolf's contribution to the speech Leighton was preparing consisted of the words mine, mate, claim, and not much else.

Leighton headed inside and to the kitchen for a quick breakfast before he found Dani and spent some time alone with her. Between the heightened patrols and Dani's task, there might not be a quiet moment to talk about his feelings for quite some time.

CHAPTER FOURTEEN

DANIELLE stretched her arms up over her head and pointed her toes as she slowly woke. She rolled over and pressed her hand down on the empty side of the bed. Leighton must have slipped out earlier in the morning. Sweet male, letting her sleep after exhausting her with some of the best sex she had ever had. Her fantasies hadn't done justice to an evening in bed with Leighton. He was insatiable.

She pulled the blanket up over her head and curled up in a ball. If she stayed in Leighton's bed, the others wouldn't find her and she could stay hidden under the covers.

The night before, Finley came knocking a few minutes after Leighton promised her a second round. Finley didn't bother waiting for Leighton to invite him in before opening the door, then almost broke an ankle turning around with his eyes closed. Not that Finley saw anything,

Leighton pulled the sheet up over them both. However, that didn't stop Leighton's wolf from showing himself and snarling at Finley.

Torn between embarrassment and not wanting to see Leighton's wolf shred a packmate, Danielle calmed both Leighton and his wolf down with a touch.

Unfortunately, embarrassment rampaged through her as Leighton walked her into the kitchen. Either the pack already knew what had happened or Finley shared everything he saw after delivering the message that the pack was waiting for them so they could continue with the meeting. She did her best to ignore the knowing looks from Eleanor and Vixen and the good-natured teasing the other males gave Leighton.

By the end of the night, patrols had been set, plans made, and Vixen and the General gave Danielle a task. She was supposed to set up a system that caught any calls or messages on the Internet about shifters, then sent her a notification. With Vixen's help, Danielle would then analyze the intercept and decide whether they needed to act.

Despite pop culture's belief that computers were all-knowing, Danielle knew Vixen and the General might as well have given her all twelve of Hercules's Labors. Like an idiot, she agreed when she got carried away with the Pack's enthusiasm. Now, in the light of day, reality hit her like a cold shower. If she stayed hidden away, she wouldn't need to confess the task was impossible.

Danielle rolled around the bed, wrapping herself up in the sheet and blanket. Leighton's room wasn't all that different from hers. Except her room had an en suite bathroom. Leighton shared a bathroom outside his room and down the hall. When she tried to convince Leighton that maybe she should go back to her room after the meeting, he had been adamant that she stay with him in his room and then proceeded to give a physical demonstration as to why staying in his bed was the better option.

A soft rustling came from the closed door and Danielle peeked out from beneath the sheet and blanket.

"Yeah?"

The door creaked open and a tow-headed little boy pushed his head through the opening. Inquisitive blue eyes peered at her without blinking. Normally, someone staring at her freaked Danielle the hell out, but this someone was three-feet tall and had a mop of blond hair with a few strands that stuck up from the back of his head.

Danielle blinked a few times and looked back at the little face staring up at her. "Foster?"

"Yep?"

"What are you doing here?"

The kid took the question to be an invitation and padded into the room, then crawled up into bed with Danielle. "Mommy and Daddy's room is locked. Why are you in Uncle Leighton's room?"

He didn't explain what Foster was doing in Leighton's room, but she shrugged it off. Plus, if Foster didn't answer her question then she didn't need to answer his. At that moment, explaining to a four-year-old the intricacies of what she was to Leighton seemed too daunting this early in the morning. Especially since she didn't even know what she meant to Leighton.

She dropped her head back on the pillow, closed her eyes, and made a mental note to lock her door before going to bed that night. Foster plopped down next to her legs and continued to stare at her.

Yep. She was locking whatever door she slept behind from here on out.

Too bad the General confiscated her phone. She had a bunch of games on it and no problem letting the kid spend the morning staring at a screen. Especially if it meant she'd get more time alone with her thoughts. Not that being alone with her thoughts was always a good thing, but it was better than a curious four-year-old's questions. Ten minutes, one question, and one hundred why's later, Danielle rolled out of bed.

She picked up her pair of pants still on the floor from the night before and pulled them on under the shirt Leighton gave her. "Come on, let's go see if we can find a box of sugar cereal I can feed you."

Danielle wasn't feeling generous towards Jackson and Eleanor. Or any of the other grown-ups who all locked their doors when they went to bed.

"Yippee!" Foster pumped the air with his little fist and led the charge down the hallway to the kitchen.

"Did I just get played?" Danielle asked her question to no one in particular.

"Probably." Leighton grinned at her and pushed a box of Cheerios across the table.

It wasn't the sweetened cereal she planned for, but she could always add sugar to it. Lots of sugar. She grabbed two bowls from the cabinet, two spoons from the drawer, and the bag of sugar from the pantry. After only a few days, she felt more comfortable moving around the pack's kitchen than her own. Once back at the table, she added cereal, milk, and sugar to one bowl, which she handed off to Foster before making her own bowl of cereal.

"You're up early." Danielle shoveled a spoonful into her mouth and crunched down on the little circles before the milk broke through their surface and turned them to mush.

"I needed a run."

"Can I come with you next time, Uncle Leighton? I promise I'll be good." Foster interjected himself into the conversation.

"Maybe."

Danielle ate another bite of cereal. Leighton wore jeans and a tight tee shirt that showed off more of his defined muscles than it hid. He must have meant running as a wolf instead of the human definition of a run. She knew there was something more hidden behind his truncated answers, but couldn't say if Leighton was being quiet because of Foster's proximity or it was just who Leighton was.

Danielle leaned to the latter.

Foster lifted his bowl to his mouth and drank up the super-sweetened milk. "Can I see Hampstead now?"

"Hmm?" Danielle looked over at the little boy. "Yeah, sure. Just don't open the cage door, okay? He's great at escaping and it will take forever to find him if he gets out."

She had planned on heading back to her room and taking a long shower before sitting down in front of the computers Vixen showed her last night.

Danielle figured she'd have to put a day into the project before admitting defeat, then convincing Vixen and General Jesup it was an impossible task. With Foster visiting Hampstead, there was no way she'd have a chance for a nice relaxing shower. At least not in the bathroom in her room.

Danielle sighed and shook her head. That left one option. And it wasn't a terrible option, either. She propped her elbows on the table and her chin on her folded hands as she gazed across the table at Leighton. "So..."

"Yeah?"

"Have you taken a shower yet this morning?"

"No." Leighton narrowed his eyes at her and tilted his head to the side.

"Want to join me? Foster will be in my room for a while, so that leaves your shower, right?"

His head tilted to the other side as he considered her suggestion. Before he over-thought the question, Danielle pushed away from the table and brought their dishes to the sink where she rinsed them and put them in the dishwasher. Once she returned everything to its proper place, she came back to the table and stretched her arm out to Leighton. With a wiggle of her fingers and a tilt of her head toward the hallway, she invited him to accompany her.

Leighton stared at her fingers, then shifted his gaze up to her eyes.

Danielle sighed, but didn't say anything. She would wait for as long as Leighton needed before he decided to join her.

From what she'd learned about him through her totally not stalker-ish research and the conversations she'd had with him, Leighton wasn't a talker. But then that was to be expected. It didn't take an advanced degree or years of therapy to realize Leighton didn't have a problem with relationships, he had a problem with *close* relationships. But that was okay since Danielle did too.

Talking, and taking showers with someone else, required a close relationship, or a closer relationship at least. Danielle hadn't ever slept in the same bed with someone (until last night) or had long conversations about life and dreams. Working for the Company made those things challenging, and Danielle had never met anyone worth the challenge. Not even her parents. Which was depressing when she thought about it, so she tried not to dwell on the subject.

Now that she was no longer part of the Company, and fate tossed her into a world that didn't care about the secrets she had once had to keep, Danielle could experience a close relationship without any hassles. And the perfect candidate for exploring a closer relationship just so happened to be part of Broken Peak Pack, the same pack Vixen was part of, who just so happened to decide that she needed to protect Danielle. Yeah, she knew the logic was roundabout, but it was still logic. That was all she needed. Well, that and an extreme amount of patience.

A random thought barreled into her mind while she prepared to stand in the middle of the kitchen with her arm out for as long as it took. "Hey, where's my P1800?"

"Your what?"

"My car? The General and I left it in the clearing before walking down that trail and meeting you. What happened to it?" Danielle took a deep quivering breath. The type of breath taken right before someone completely lost their shit and went into full panic mode.

"Oh, that," Leighton shrugged. "Not sure, Jackson or Roose moved it. Probably to the same place as Eleanor's Explorer."

"And where's that?" Leighton's explanation did nothing to ease Danielle's growing panic. If anything, her anxiety doubled. "There's not much I have in this world that I can say is mine, but my car is one of them. My parents and I aren't close, but I had my grandma. After Grammy died, my parents sold off her estate, but she left her P1800 to me because she knew I loved it. It's the only thing I have left of my grandmother."

Leighton's eyes turned silver as he jumped to his feet and stalked toward Danielle. "We have a storage barn where we keep vehicles. I'm sure it's there."

Danielle closed her eyes and inhaled a deep, steadying breath. "You're sure?"

"I'm sure it is, Dani, but we can check on it later if you want." Leighton pressed his hand down on her shoulder for a moment before jerking it away as though her skin burned his hand.

Danielle didn't experience any burning, but with his touch, a shock ran through her body setting all of her nerve endings to tingle mode. She shuddered, but couldn't deny enjoying the sensations. The charge reminded Danielle she was still alive. Something she couldn't say she'd experienced in a long time. Although, to be fair, the jolt of feeling alive and present in the world might have also been caused by the near panic attack.

"I want." She offered him a tentative smile before pulling her bottom lip between her teeth.

They stood facing one another for several minutes. Leighton stared at Danielle and Danielle rubbed her knuckles along her sternum in a futile attempt to lower her heart rate.

Finally, Leighton spoke, filling the silence with a low rumbling voice. "When I came here, I didn't have anything that was mine. When we were younger, Bray utilized the hand-me-down method for keeping us clothed. We shared everything."

"You never had anything that was just yours?"

"Nope," Leighton shook his head, "at least not until Vixen arrived. She gave me a knife."

Danielle's arm dropped to her side. "The knife you handed me?"

Leighton nodded.

Danielle grinned and bobbed her head along with him. "Did we just share?"

"I guess. Come on," he reached for her hand and entwined his fingers with hers. "Let's take a shower and then we'll go visit your car."

"We can bring your knife too. That way we can introduce your knife to my car."

Leighton snorted, "you're weird."

"Yeah. But that's because most of my conversations up to now have been with people I haven't ever met face to face."

He tugged her into a bathroom and reached around her to close the door. She heard the familiar sound of a lock clicking into place.

Leighton offered an explanation, although he didn't need to. "Foster considers all unlocked doors an open invitation to come in and explore."

Danielle had visited the bathroom, but hadn't spent much time looking at it. It only took a few moments of a cursory examination for Leighton's words about not having anything to hit her full on. The bathroom could have belonged to anyone. Same for the rest of the lodge, as the pack members called the house. There was nothing personal in any of the rooms, not even Leighton's bedroom. Well, a few items had Tevin's name written on them in indelible ink, but it didn't stop anyone from using them.

The fridge had personal items, but those were all pictures Foster had drawn.

She hadn't seen Eleanor and Jackson's or Foster's rooms. Maybe they had more personal touches?

The idea of personal decorating touches abruptly left Danielle's thoughts and were immediately replaced with the idea of personal touches of a different type. While Danielle had been lost in her thoughts, Leighton had been busy. He turned the shower on and had pulled off his clothes. Danielle had seen Leighton in several states of undress, but somehow, seeing him in his current state was jaw-dropping.

In a good way.

Danielle stared at Leighton's faded bruises and the clear definition of his muscles beneath the tanned skin of someone who spent a lot of time outside. While the view preoccupied her, Leighton reached down and lifted her shirt until she raised her arms so he could pull it off. Before her shirt even hit the ground, he had her pants unfastened and pulled off.

When Leighton stood back up, Danielle lifted her gaze to the ceiling and studied the tiny crack where the walls met at the corner.

Leighton chuckled as he led her into the shower with him, "you were the one who invited me to shower, Dani."

"Yeah, but that was before I considered the logistics." She kept her gaze locked on the ceiling.

The ceiling was a safer target than staring at the monster between Leighton's legs. He turned her around so her back was to his chest and she lowered her gaze. The move didn't go unnoticed by Leighton and his chuckle changed into a laugh.

"You'll have to do some work today, right?" Leighton stepped under the water and brought Danielle with him, getting her hair wet.

"Yeah. Once I get an alert system set up, I'll have to go out and make sure the receivers are installed in the right locations. Although what they want me to do and what I'm capable of doing are two separate things." She bent her head back and closed her eyes as the water sluiced through her purple colored hair. Hair dye would have to be added to a shopping list if she stayed at Broken Peak. Either that or she'd have to learn to live with blond roots while the color grew out.

Leighton added shampoo to her hair and massaged his fingers against her scalp.

Danielle groaned, "how are you so good at that?"

"At what?" Leighton sounded distracted.

"Washing hair."

"We've all had to wash Foster's wolf at some point. His pup finds some of the worst things to roll around in. After the first few tries, we learned his pup tolerates baths when we take the time to massage him."

"That's both sweet and weird." She stepped backwards with Leighton's help until her head was under the water and rinsed the shampoo from her hair. "What about you? Do you have to patrol tonight?"

"Not tonight no, but I will have to patrol in the late afternoon. If we visit your car this morning, will that give you enough time to set up the system before I have to head out?"

"It should. Why?"

"My wolf wants me to go with you when you set up the receivers."

As the soap ran from her hair and circled around the drain, Danielle turned, wiping her hair back with the palms of her hands. "Your wolf?"

"Me too." The corner of Leighton's mouth quirked up. He set his hands on her shoulders and spun them around so he faced the shower and she stayed under the spray. "I guess we're protective of what's ours."

"I'm yours?" She wrapped her arms around his waist and set her head against his chest while he was busy washing his hair and couldn't push her away.

"Yeah. You've been mine since the first time I saw you tottering down the path in those stupid shoes of yours. I just hadn't figured it out. After last night, though? Pushing you away isn't going to work for either of us."

Danielle tilted her head back and blinked up at Leighton, who refused to look down at her the same way she had refused to look down when he undressed her. She brushed her fingertips across his chest and over his shoulder. Most of his wounds had faded as if days had passed and not hours, except the mark on the top of his shoulder.

She pushed up on her toes and examined the wound. "Did I do that? How come it hasn't healed like the bruises?"

"Yes you did, little miss bitey." His knuckles brushed over her cheek as he spun them back around so he could rinse the shampoo from his hair. "It will fade in time, unless I mark you too. We figured it out with Jackson and Eleanor. Her mark on him faded until he marked her. But don't worry. I won't claim you."

"Not even if I want you to?"

"Not until I'm sure you want me to." Leighton turned off the water and reached past the shower curtain for a towel. He dried her body first, taking his time to pamper her before rubbing the towel over her body. "Put my shirt back on and make a dash for my room. I'll get you some clothes."

"I can just go back to my room."

Leighton growled, "no you can't. Someone might see you."

"In your shirt? It practically hits my knees."

His eyes flashed silver, and he gave her a toothy grin. "Humor my wolf."

Danielle harrumphed, but did as Leighton asked.

She sat down on the edge of his bed and waited for him to return with clothes for her. She wondered if she'd have to run back to her room and change again. Leighton didn't have the best fashion sense considering the clothes he packed for her when he picked up Hampstead.

CHAPTER FIFTEEN

"ARE you done yet?" Leighton paced the width of the computer room Danielle had dubbed mission control.

Vixen had been busy and a stack of computers, monitors, hard drives, and everything else that any good technophile had on their dream list awaited Danielle. Maybe the task Vixen and general Jessup gave her wouldn't be impossible. Definitely difficult, but not completely impossible. Somehow, Vixen gathered items that were still in prototype stages. Or at least Danielle hadn't seen them on the market yet.

Danielle's fingers flew across the keyboard as she put in the final lines of code that would pair the receivers with the basic program she set up in the system to alert them when anyone from Unit D, who still carried the technology Danielle tweaked, came within three miles of the receivers. "A few more minutes."

"You said that ten minutes ago. What are you doing?"

She sighed, closed her eyes, and counted to five. Leighton asked more questions than Foster. "I need to make sure my program can interpret the signals from the receivers or the walk in the woods we take will be a complete waste of time."

Leighton resumed pacing and Danielle continued pounding the keyboard. Inviting him to come and watch her work after they visited her car in a storage barn that served double duty as an automotive museum in another life made the top ten list of poor decisions, right behind getting into a cage with a mountain lion.

With a final flourish of her fingers across the keys, Danielle spun her chair around and looked up at the still pacing Leighton. "Done. Or at least mostly done."

He stopped on a dime and pivoted before dropping to his knees between her thighs. Leighton rested his hands on her knees. "Really?"

Danielle ran her fingers through his almost too long hair and smiled. "Really."

Leighton hopped to his feet and grabbed the canvas rucksack already packed with the receivers. She gave him the packing task five minutes into his pacing, thinking it would distract him. The distraction lasted for all of three minutes before he was back to walking back and forth. If only everyone she worked with had been as efficient as Leighton.

"Okay, let's go, woman."

Danielle leaned back in her swiveling office chair, the expensive kind made from mesh that cradled her body. Vixen spared no expense outfitting Danielle's workspace. With her arms on the armrests and her legs stretched out in front of her and crossed at the ankles, she studied the massive man, he was still very much a man to her since she hadn't yet seen his wolf, hopping from foot to foot in front of her.

"What?" He pushed his hair out of his eyes.

"Why are you so impatient to go outside?"

Leighton averted his gaze and pushed his hands into his pockets. "I want to show you something."

Danielle sat up straight and bounced up and down in her chair. She clapped her hands together and squealed. "What are we going to see? The waterfall? Oh wait, do you have a secret hiding place? Wait, you have a den, right?"

He pulled his hands from his pockets and reached down for her, pulling her to her feet as she rambled off all the different places she thought he might take her to. Leighton slung the bag over his shoulder then tossed a heavy sweater at her. "Put this on."

She caught the heavy wool, barely, and held it to her chest. Danielle smelled Leighton on the sweater and took a deep breath. She knew better than to believe a male like Leighton would wear cologne, but he had a distinct scent. A combination of the outdoors and pine and something sweet that she couldn't place, like honey. "Why?"

"Do you ever do anything anyone asks you to do without asking questions? It's cool outside and I don't want you to get a chill. If we want to have enough time to do everything I want, we need to leave before something else distracts you."

She nodded and pulled the sweater over her head and down over the three blouses she had on. Leighton hadn't liked how easy it was to see through the thin fabric and ran back to her room for more shirts. The sweater sleeves hung down well past her hands and the bottom hit further down her legs than some of her skirts and dresses. She comprehended Leighton's size at a practical level, even when he stood in front of her. But when she wore something of his, just how big he was hit her full on. At least two of her could fit in his sweater without stretching it out. Probably even three of her.

By the time she rolled up the sleeves, Leighton was walking out the door and down the hallway. She hurried after him while pulling her hair back in a messy bun on the top of her head. In the front room, they passed Foster reading his favorite book about Pete the Cat, who had somehow turned into a wolf according to Foster's version.

Leighton shrugged his shoulder, so the rucksack was obvious. "We're putting up the receivers."

Finley glanced up then gave Leighton a chin lift and Danielle a wink with a wide grin. "Whatever. Have fun storming the castle."

In the way of most children when they found something particularly funny, Foster laughed louder and harder than absolutely necessary at the film reference. Apparently, it was his favorite movie, and he loved to retell it to anyone he managed to hold captive for just a few minutes. It was hard to say no to the boy. Hence why Danielle had already heard three different versions of *The Princess Bride*.

She raced around Leighton and opened the door before stepping outside into the cool afternoon air before Foster wrangled Leighton and her into another retelling. Leighton was right behind her. He rested his palm against the small of her back and guided her across the yard to where the trees met the grass.

"You're not what I expected," Leighton whispered as he led her into the woods.

"And just what did you expect?" Danielle stopped at the wood's edge and planted her hands on her hips. "Wait, what do you mean by expected. Coming here wasn't planned, how did you find out about it to have enough time to have an expectation?"

"That's not what I meant, Dani." Leighton rolled his eyes and slipped his hand from her back to her wrist, pulling her along behind him. "The first I heard of your arrival was when Vixen told me to come with them to meet you."

"Oh. Then what did you mean?" She pulled her bottom lip between her teeth. Sometimes it felt like she and Leighton were speaking different languages.

"What have you learned about mates from your research?"

"Um, nothing. Unless you count the Romance novels, and I figured those authors just had really good imaginations."

Leighton kept them walking deeper into the forest. "I wouldn't know. I've never read any."

"Really? Oh my God, You really should have someone scouring every new paranormal Romance that comes out just to see how close to the truth they are."

"Has anyone ever told you that having a conversation with you can be difficult."

"No. I'm an excellent conversationalist, thank you."

"When you aren't jumping from topic to topic you are. Can we go back to my question or do you want to talk about books some more?"

Danielle sighed, "we can go back to your original question."

"All right. So what do you know about mates?"

"Um, that Vixen is Bray's mate and Eleanor is Jackson's."

"That's it?" Leighton stopped and spun to face her. "In all your research and studying, that's all you learned?"

She yanked her hand back and stared up at him with her mouth open. "All my research started back with Vixen and was all about keeping your pack safe. Learning about mates didn't help and despite my phone, which the General confiscated by the way, being filled with enough ebooks to get me through the end of the world, I didn't take notes on fictional mates."

The corner of Leighton's mouth lifted in a hint of a smile and he raised his hands in surrender. "Fair enough. Here's some firsthand information for your research then. Shifters choose mates we're stuck with for the rest of our lives. Once our wolf chooses, that's it. As long as we don't make the mating official with a claiming, our animal will remain mildly obsessed. Once the bond gets locked in place when the male claims his mate, both the animal and the male can become extremely obsessive."

"Just males?" The confession should have scared the hell out of Danielle. A world filled with supernatural stalkers with above average strength and senses didn't bode well for any human women who caught the eye of a shifter's animal. "Oh. Ohhh. Oh my God! So are wolf packs a whole patriarchal misogynistic mess?"

"What? No!" Leighton shook his head, but didn't hide his small smile. "In most cases the feeling is mutual, but sometimes it's one-sided. When that happens, most will keep their distance."

"Most?"

"My father didn't. He claimed my mother. I'm not the product of a loving couple, like Vixen and Bray or Jackson and Eleanor."

Danielle stepped closer to Leighton. She wanted to hug him and tell him how sorry she was for him, but he seemed like the type of guy who would see it as pity and resent her. "Not everyone's family is like *Leave it to Beaver*. Most families aren't. Almost every family has a load of problems they keep hidden away."

"Dani, a one-sided mating for my kind is worse than dysfunctional. My father was jealous of any attention my mother gave me."

"Any?" Danielle bit down on the inside of her bottom lip to keep from revealing what she had dug up on Leighton when she shouldn't have been looking.

"All of it. And when she wasn't there anymore, that was my fault."

"You realize I'm going to tell you it's not your fault, right?"

"Vixen said the same thing, but it's easy to say it's not my fault if you aren't living it."

Danielle shrugged, "my parents ignored me. I wasn't neglected, but it was like I didn't exist in their world. Everyone always told me it wasn't my fault. I might not have accepted it at the time, but eventually, after I don't know how many times I was told it wasn't my fault, I believed it. Maybe if we say it enough times, you'll believe it wasn't your fault too."

"That's not my point."

She grinned, "I know, but like you said, having a linear conversation with me is difficult."

"I didn't say that."

"But you meant it. Okay, so if your animal decides someone's their mate, they obsess if it's not reciprocated."

Leighton pulled his eyebrows together and his forehead crinkled. "Yeah."

"Leighton, why are you telling me this?"

"Because I knew my wolf would eventually choose a mate and bond. It's one of the reasons why I haven't left Broken Peak except for the occasional visits to town. If I only leave for short periods of time, I don't have to worry about someday seeing my mate and then my wolf obsessing about her until I turn into my father and claim her, even if she doesn't want it."

The pieces clicked into place. Granted, Danielle didn't have much experience with shifters and what she knew came from a combination of podcasts, websites, and the messages from Vixen, but she should have seen it sooner.

Leighton did everything to keep his distance, but when instinct took over, he only wanted to be close to her.

Hell, she'd even bitten him. *Hard.* At the time she didn't understand where the urge came from, she hadn't exactly made it a practice to bite her partners.

She wasn't what he expected...

Holy shit!

Holy double shit!

"Say it." Danielle lifted her chin, crossed her arms over her chest, and narrowed her eyes at him. As much as she might believe something to be true, she still needed to hear the words from him. "Just say it."

"You aren't who I expected my mate to be." He closed his eyes and turned his head to the side before opening them again and staring off into the woods. "I tried, Dani, I tried to keep away from you, but I couldn't and I don't want to."

"Then don't." Danielle stepped next to Leighton and laced her fingers through his. "Show me what you wanted me to see."

He looked down at her and lifted their clasped hands so they both saw the way his hand swallowed hers and her fingers wove together with his. With a slow exhale, Leighton let their hands drop, but didn't let go of her as he continued along the barely visible trail. "You aren't the kind of female I thought my wolf wanted, but I'm glad he chose you."

"Most girls would think that means you didn't choose me, that some outside force picked me, so it wasn't your choice." She grinned at him and bumped her shoulder against his arm.

"You aren't most girls, Dani." He stared straight ahead, keeping his eyes on the path so he wouldn't have to look at her.

"Now, there you go saying something sweet." She squeezed his hand and leaned against him as they walked.

Danielle rolled her eyes, "take the compliment, Leighton."

Leighton stopped in a small clearing and turned toward her. He slipped the rucksack off his shoulder then handed it to her. His hands found her waist, and he lifted her up, setting her back down on a large rock, or small boulder. It could go either way. He stepped away from her and toed off his boots. His hands reached behind his back and pulled up his shirt. Before he pulled it off, his arms fell to his sides.

"The attacks will get worse, won't they?"

Danielle tilted her head from side to side. "Wellll…"

"Does dragging the word out longer than necessary make it mean something new?"

"No. But no one wants the answer to your question to be yes. I went with a word that could mean yes with the right inflections." The reason made perfect sense in her mind. "Unit D is sort of independent because the government can't acknowledge they have a team of elite assassins who might also run the occasional rescue mission, but are mostly trained killers. So, I guess it depends."

"Depends on what?"

"On who's the higher power. If they resent Vixen and the General, then it's going to get a lot worse. If Vixen continues to antagonize them, a whole lot worse. If Vixen manages to scare the shit out of them, it will probably get less worse until they find something bigger and badder than her. Or, it might all end in a war between humans and shifters."

Leighton blinked at her. "We can't ever let the others know."

"Know what? How bad it's going to get?"

"No, that you have the answers Vixen doesn't like to share until Bray forces her to."

Danielle laughed at the image of the pack firing off one question after another.

"Don't laugh. I'm serious. Finley and Jackson will follow you around like Foster follows the adults around." A smile accompanied Leighton's warning.

She kicked her heels against the side of the rock and leaned back on one hand so she could use her free hand to give him a beckoning wave. "You were in the middle of something before you asked your question. Maybe you should continue?"

Leighton shook his head at her suggestion, but did as she asked. His hands found the back collar of his shirt and pulled it up over his head, then dropped it to the ground by his boots.

Danielle's eyes widened at the half-naked male in front of her. It never ceased to amaze her that there wasn't a gym in sight, but all the males had the muscle definition of players in the NFL.

Oh. She definitely had to dig into some of the files on NFL players once she got the rest of her network up and running and safe behind hundreds of layers of security.

"Um, not that I'm unappreciative of your little show, because it truly is amazing, but why are you taking off your clothes to put up the receivers?" Danielle lifted the rucksack in her lap and swung it at him by the straps. "I'm sure I told you that the receivers have to go up in the trees and last I checked, climbing trees half naked is going to be problematic."

"We'll do the receivers after." Leighton's fingers unbuttoned his jeans and pulled the zipper down. They fell to his ankles, and he kicked them over to his shirt and boots and stood in front of her naked.

"After?" Danielle looked over Leighton's shoulder. She'd seen it all before, but that had been in a bedroom. In the dark. And the bathroom before a shower. This? A naked Leighton in the middle of the day in the middle of the forest would make it easier for Leighton to notice her obvious staring. "Leighton, if you wanted to have sex, we didn't have to leave the lodge. I'm sure the chair could have supported us. Maybe try out an office fantasy or something?"

Leighton closed his eyes and shook his head. "Dani."

"What? I really don't like the idea of the General or Vixen stumbling upon us. Or worse, what if Foster goes for a walk?"

"Dani, we aren't making love out here. My wolf couldn't handle the possibility of anyone seeing you uncovered and I don't much like the idea either."

"Then why are you taking off your clothes?"

"Dani," Leighton growled, "weren't you listening? I told you I wanted to show you something."

"But I've already seen your dick. We didn't need to come out here for you to show it to me again." Danielle covered her eyes with her palm.

"Woman, we aren't in the woods so we could play a game of I'll show you mine and you show me yours."

"Are you showing me your wolf?" Danielle's eyes bugged out her head as she pulled her palm away so she could clap her hands in glee. Her entire body shook. In her brief time at Broken Peak, she hadn't seen any of the wolves. She caught a glimpse of Jackson once, and Foster a few times, but the animals stayed away from her. Plus, she didn't feel it was appropriate to call a wolf over like it was a dog.

She forgot about Leighton's nudity and slipped down off the boulder. Careful of the receivers in the rucksack, she slung it over her shoulders. Once she secured the bag, she bounced around him and grinned. She was actually going to see his wolf.

Leighton pressed his thumb and middle finger against his temples and shook his head. The head shaking might have been caused by frustration, but she didn't care. Danielle was going to see his wolf. She couldn't stop bouncing and her hands hadn't paused once since she started clapping.

There was his growl again. The noise sent tingles all over her body. On an upward bounce, Leighton grabbed Danielle by the waist and put her back on the rock.

"Can I pet him? Will he let me pet him? I wanna pet him. I bet he loves belly rubs! And ear scritches."

"Dani, stay put. Until he's had a chance to meet you. And no, you can't pet him and whatever else. He's not a dog, Dani, he's a wolf. Not just an enormous wolf, but a gigantic wolf. He's not a pet like your hamster."

"Oh? What if Hampstead is a shifter?"

"He's not."

"How can you be sure?"

"I just am. Do you want to meet my wolf or not? Because it's all I can do to keep him from tearing out of my skin."

Danielle raised a finger, holding off Leighton's next comment. "We're going to table that whole you can tell shifters from not shifters for later, because I have a lot of questions, but yes, I want to meet your wolf."

Leighton grinned and winked. "Are you sure?"

"Yes, I'm sure. Sheesh, no wonder Finley is Foster's favorite uncle."

Leighton rolled his eyes. "Finley is Foster's favorite uncle because Finley gives Foster everything he asks for."

Danielle smiled. Yeah, Leighton's assessment was right, but it was still fun teasing him. She was about to say as much when the man standing in front of her was gone.

No bright flash of light. No loud noise. Not even a burst of sparkles, which Danielle found slightly disappointing.

The shift was almost instantaneous. A mere blink of her eyes and instead of avoiding looking at a naked man's dick, Danielle stared at a silver-eyed absolutely gigantic golden furred (or was it haired) wolf.

Leighton wasn't wrong when he said his wolf wasn't just a large wolf. Sitting on top of the rock, Danielle figured the top of her head would hit close to the six foot mark. The wolf's head would have hit her chest if he moved closer. That made him close to five feet at the shoulders.

Five. Huge. Fucking. Feet.

Holy hell, Leighton's wolf was enormous.

All caution went with the wind and Danielle jumped down to the ground. The words spilled out of her mouth with her rising excitement. "Oh my God, you are ginormous! And cute. But don't tell Leighton I said that. Can I pet you? Leighton said you aren't a pet, but I bet you're soft."

The wolf sat down and twisted his head clockwise, as though he understood every single word. Or maybe Leighton was translating for her. She'd have to remember to ask him about it when he shifted back.

Danielle lost her fight with her self-control. She reached out to the wolf and scratched the spot between his ears. He was so massive, she didn't even have to reach down. The wolf closed his eyes under her ministrations.

"You are such a big boy! And you are soft. Just like I thought! Wait until I tell Leighton."

The wolf opened his eyes and instead of the silver she expected to see, Leighton's blue eyes gazed at her.

"Okaaay, so I don't have to tell him, he already heard. This is so cool." She wasn't talking to the wolf as much as she was talking to herself, but the wolf didn't seem to mind.

The wolf stood and pushed her towards Leighton's clothes. Leighton might not be able to talk to her in this form, but he could still communicate. She picked up the discarded jeans and shirt, folded them, and placed them in the rucksack with the receivers and his boots.

The wolf alternated between watching her and scanning the woods. As soon as the rucksack hung from her shoulders, Leighton huffed out a loud sigh then turned and walked to the opposite path from where they entered the grove. Before he disappeared into the woods, he stopped and waited. He didn't want her walking behind him. She approached the wolf and placed her hand on his back.

"See, you don't need words at all, your wolf and I are on the same wavelength! Oh, wolflength. We're on the same wolflength! I made a new word. Eleanor is going to have to add it to her research."

The wolf huffed at her.

Danielle's cheeks hurt from smiling. The revelation that Leighton could still talk to her, even without a voice, made her incredibly happy. Whatever doubts she might have had about Leighton and her disappeared in that moment. She just wished Leighton had the same thought.

CHAPTER SIXTEEN

"YOUR paws are as big as my feet." Danielle looked down at the ground so she wouldn't trip over anything and relied on Leighton to stop her from running into a tree or rock.

The wolf chuffed, but continued walking. As long as her hand remained on his back, he kept moving. Whenever she lifted her hand off him, the wolf would stop and sit, waiting patiently for her hand to return. The third time she tested his reaction, she continued walking. Leighton bit down on the rucksack and pulled her back next to him.

Her free hand took on a mind of its own and before she realized what she was doing, Danielle compared her index finger to his canine. "Holy Crap, Leighton, your teeth are bigger than my fingers!"

While they walked, Danielle entertained herself by comparing different body parts with his. Fingers and teeth, feet and paws, fingernails and claws, arm length and tail length. The wolf seemed to tolerate her running commentary, and she might even have amused him.

She wasn't entirely sure how long they'd been walking when they came up to the river's edge. In the distance, she heard the roar of what must have been a waterfall, but the water in front of them was slow moving and clear.

Too bad it was cold, it would have been a nice place to swim.

Danielle added another goal to her to-do list: Stay around long enough to go swimming in the river.

The wolf stopped and pulled away from her. He circled the area until he found a spot with plenty of grass and leaves and not nearly as much sand. For the second time, The wolf pulled Danielle into the place the wolf (or maybe it was Leighton) wanted her. But he had found her a comfortable place to sit down, so she didn't complain. She slipped the rucksack off and set it against a nearby tree.

The wolf sat next to her and leaned against her. Danielle wrapped her arm around his back and pressed her cheek to his shoulder.

"So, I guess Leighton is still inside there and can hear whatever I say. I am also guessing you can hear and understand me too." Danielle decided to treat Leighton's wolf and Leighton as two separate entities, even if she believed they shared more than the space they inhabited.

The wolf turned his head toward her and licked her nose.

"Ew, wolf drool!" Danielle wiped her hand across her face.

The wolf responded by butting his head against her shoulder and chest and pushing Danielle until she fell to her back. Leighton flopped down next to her and rested his head on her stomach.

Danielle looked up at the sky and stroked the soft fur along the top of the wolf's nose. The large branches from the ancient trees formed a canopy over their heads. The wind pushed the white clouds across the blue backdrop, disappearing behind the thick branches for a few seconds before reappearing in the next opening.

She couldn't remember the last time she spent even a few minutes gazing at clouds. Her life, especially after joining the Company, had been structured and scheduled to the second. She hadn't taken lunch in she didn't know how many years. And when she was at home, work wasn't far from her mind.

That hadn't changed since running away to Broken Peak, except the priorities had shifted. Instead of worrying about agents keeping their covers, she fretted about the safety of Foster and his extended family.

The clouds didn't share in those worries. They happily moved along, altering their shape until the puffs formed something recognizable to the human mind. Mostly sailboats and ice cream scoops.

Despite danger looming over Danielle and the pack and uncertainty leering at them from an ever-closing distance, Leighton gave Danielle a moment of peacefulness.

Leighton sighed. A noise similar to the sound Leighton the male made, but unique to the wolf.

"Did you use meeting your wolf as an excuse for me to take a break?"

Leighton lifted his head and turned to face her. With each blink of his eyes, the color flashed from silver to blue.

"You and Leighton are sneaky, wolf." Danielle pressed up on her elbows. "I work hard. I always have. And with this project they gave me, I'll probably never leave my computers. Do me a favor? Take me outside every now and then to look up at the sky."

Leighton belly crawled closer to her and laid his head down on her chest. She scratched his ears and kissed the tip of his nose. "I'm taking that as a yes. Thank you."

Danielle flopped back down and resumed watching the clouds.

They stayed like that, wolf and woman, for a few more minutes. Then, just like in the clearing, the wolf and man switched places in a blink of an eye. No noise. No light. One minute a wolf was pressing his head to her chest and the next Leighton was looking up at her.

"I think my wolf likes you."

"Well, that's good, because I like your wolf."

"We all have places our animals like to hide. Mine's pretty territorial and he doesn't like the others coming here. You're the first person he's allowed to visit."

She combed her fingers through his hair. "I hope both of you let me visit again sometime."

As she looked back up at the sky and the clouds, a wandering thought ran through her mind like someone dressed in one of those tyrannosaurus costumes with the tiny arms. Leighton was still naked. Completely, bare-assed naked. And he was lying half on top of her.

The giggles hit and she couldn't stop herself. They started small, her shoulders shaking as she tried to keep the noise from escaping.

She wasn't successful.

"What's so funny?"

"You. Well, not you, more you're bare-assed naked, but you aren't a bear. So, does that make you wolf-assed naked?"

"Dani," Leighton shook his head at her observation, but didn't bother hiding his smile.

"What? It's true. Sort of."

Leighton planted his fists on either side of her head and pushed up. Danielle stared at the way his muscles rippled with the movement and wondered if they were far enough away from the Lodge to not get caught.

"What are you doing?"

"We need to get the receivers put up, right?" Leighton rolled away from her and pulled his clothes from the rucksack.

While he dressed, Danielle stared up at the sky and promised herself she wouldn't forget that Leighton's wolf brought her to his place. "Does it hurt?"

Leighton's face appeared above her, blocking her view of the sky. "Does what hurt?"

"The shifting from wolf to man or man to wolf?"

"I guess a little. But it's not really a hurt, more of being uncomfortable. Like if you're wearing clothes that are too tight."

"I have a killer pair of heels. They never fit me right, but they make my legs look amazing, so I wear them over a more comfortable pair. But that's a choice. I can't imagine living my entire life wearing those heels every day for even fifteen minutes." Danielle scrunched her nose at him, as if the slight gesture could convey all of her empathy. "Is there anything to make it better? Soaking my feet helps me."

"It's not so bad that we need to make it better or easier. It's just what it is." Leighton reached for her hand and pulled her up to her feet as though she didn't weigh more than a feather. Once she was situated in a standing position, he snatched the rucksack and slung it over his shoulder. "Do you know where you want the receivers?"

Danielle brushed the pine needles from her ass and squinted her eyes as she looked into the distance. "Not specifically, no. I have enough receivers to set up a line about a quarter mile past the official boundary of the pack territory according to the most recent survey."

"What does that mean, Dani?"

"It means we head about a half mile," she spun around until her body faced in the general direction where she wanted to begin the receiver line and pointed into the woods. "There. There's a good spot where the tree line hits the mountain. We'll start there. It will intercept any assaults from the peak and we won't have to build a complete perimeter."

Leighton cocked his head to the side and grinned at her. "You have no idea what direction to go in, do you?"

"Sure, I do. I can see the mountain."

He shook his head with a laugh. "Not at all what I expected."

"Yep, but we decided that was a good thing." Hiking the waist of her pants up over her hips, she pushed her way into the woods and headed in the general direction of the mountain.

Leighton came up behind her. He pressed his hand against her lower back and shifted her direction to her right. "If you kept on your original trajectory, you would have found yourself back at the front yard of the Lodge."

"Well that wouldn't be any good." She stretched her arm out behind her and blindly flailed her hand around until Leighton finally divined her intentions and grabbed her hand. She squeezed his fingers tight. "Do you mind this?"

"No. I thought I would, but I don't."

Danielle continued walking, but looked over her shoulder at him with a wide smile. "Ha, see, we're totally meant for each other. You didn't have to ask what you minded. You knew what I meant."

Leighton growled, but it came from the wolf inside him and was more of a grumble than a full on growl. She rather liked the way her body responded to his noises.

"Or maybe my response was generic enough for any question you intended."

"And yet you are still holding my hand."

For their entire conversation, she hadn't once looked where she was headed. But it didn't matter. Leighton made sure she didn't trip, stumble, or run into anything.

"Yes, I am. But if I let go, you'll either end up hurting yourself and I'll get yelled at by both you and Vixen, or you'll keep flailing your arm around like a fish out of water until I take your hand again."

"I prefer my theory to yours, but you are right about one thing. I don't plan on letting go anytime soon."

CHAPTER SEVENTEEN

BRIGHT green letters and numbers filled the black screens of Danielle's monitors as she worked on getting the receivers all online and communicating with the system she set up earlier in the day. While she waited for everything to fall into place, Vixen hovered behind her.

"You're worse than Leighton, you know?"

"Hardly. That boy and his wolf are so far gone for you, he couldn't leave you alone for twenty minutes. I, on the other hand, am more than capable of leaving you alone for much longer periods of time."

"Well, he's not here now, is he? You are. And breathing down my neck." She mumbled the last sentence under her breath.

"The General and I are curious about how long our project might take." Vixen flopped down in the extra office chair she sneaked in while Danielle and Leighton had been setting up the receivers and spun in circles as she stared up at the ceiling.

Danielle huffed out a sigh and blew her bangs out of her eyes. "I know what you want, but despite what the movies and TV shows portray, artificial intelligence isn't nearly as advanced as the two of you believe it is."

"I haven't watched TV or seen a movie in years." Vixen brushed away Danielle's excuse with a wave of her hand. "We don't need your program to think, just intercept different communications and pull out everything that's of interest to us."

"And where exactly are we supposed to grab these interceptions? I can't pluck them out of thin air."

"We'll get you the feeds."

Feeds only meant one thing. Vixen or the General had access, or could *gain* access, to all the data that a particular agency siphoned off from daily communications. An agency that according to the government didn't exist for many years.

Danielle wasn't sure how she felt about it.

On one hand, she wouldn't have to worry about how advanced artificial intelligence was because she just had to create a few algorithms to snatch the pertinent communications out of the feeds. On the other hand, it was never about what the agency was capable of, but who was in charge of those capabilities.

"Oh, God, Vixen, don't offer me the feeds." Danielle rubbed her palms up and down her cheeks. "That's like offering a starving man entry to an all you can eat buffet, but making him sign his soul and all his descendants' souls over to the devil."

"The General and I promise we'll never ask to see anything. Your program will decide if you should look at it then you decide if the rest of us see it. Mac will act as your confessor. If you can't decide, he can help you with the decision."

"You say that now."

"I mean it, Danielle. You'll have complete control. You can even set up a kill switch."

"Whoa," her hand shot up, "I can even set up a kill switch? A kill switch isn't a bonus here, it's a frickin' requirement. Without a kill switch, this entire conversation is a non-starter."

Vixen blinked twice. Slowly. "Foster isn't around, you can say fucking."

Danielle's jaw dropped as she blinked back at Vixen. "That's your take away?"

"No, but I figured if you felt free to curse, we might shorten the back and forth before you grudgingly tell me you'll do it with conditions that both the General and I already agree to."

"How can you ensure they won't trace it back to us, to me, if you access the feeds?" Danielle closed her eyes. Vixen was right, the temptation was too great and Danielle would eventually cave, but she had to at least give the appearance of being against the idea.

"I can't. Neither can my asset. You have to do that bit of handy work yourself. If it has to be done at the point where we drop the listening device then you'll need to walk my asset through it since you can't leave here and remain safe."

"Are you shitting me?" Danielle pressed her palm against her forehead. By the end of the conversation, she'd have a permanent indentation of her hand on her head. "Did you and the General come up with a plan that might actually give the Three Stooges a run for their money as the most ill-conceived idea of all time? This isn't a deep water cable we can attach a line to and hope no one notices it's there!"

"There's already an external feed. That's our access point. What we need you to do is make sure it can't flow back to us."

The ideas took shape in Danielle's mind. From a block of marble into Michaelangelo's David, she pictured the lines of code and the algorithms she needed for her masterpiece. "What's your exact goal? Because the way you and the General described it, you want advanced notice anytime a shifter might be in danger, and that's impossible. You understand that, right?"

"For now, but given enough time, I imagine your algorithms will predict when a shifter is in danger."

"Assuming whoever is causing them harm is communicating through phones and emails, but that's years away."

"You'll also have camera feeds."

At some point their conversation shifted from why Danielle couldn't do what Vixen and the General wanted to how she could make it work.

"Won't matter, unless you have a database full of images of shifters for facial recognition."

"Not yet, we don't."

"Not ever, Vixen. Do you know what would happen if it ever fell into the wrong hands. There can never be an image database. Never. Ever."

The ease of piggy-backing onto the feeds highlighted the vulnerability of an image database. Danielle cringed at the thought. Even a database of names could be dangerous to shifters. Sure, she could place as many protections as possible, but like Vixen used to tell Unit D, 'there's always someone smarter and badder than you in the room'. In Unit D's case, it was always Vixen. In Danielle's case, it was always someone younger who understood the power of working in the shadows and never sticking their head above the surface to gloat. No matter how good Danielle was, there would always be someone better and they would sell that information to the highest bidder.

Vixen swung the chair from side to side and gripped its arms. "Can we at least agree to keep it open for discussion?"

"I don't see how. Shit, Vixen, you of all people should understand that no system is invulnerable to someone determined to break in. They don't even have to know what they are looking for or at. The stronger the lock, the more tempting it is for someone like me."

"Then make sure someone like you can't find it. Something is coming down the road, Danielle. I don't know what it is, but both Mac and Eleanor are convinced that what you're doing here is important to us coming out alive on the other side. And that includes some kind of database or catalog of shifters as we learn about them."

Danielle turned back to her computer screens. Her fingers punched at the keyboard. There was no way she would be able to convince Vixen to give up the idea of a database, not after she had made up her mind about it already. Instead, Danielle would have to figure out a way to show Vixen why it was such a bad idea.

Vixen pushed off the chair and took the few steps to the door. She rested her hand on the handle before opening the door. "Nice job in placing the receivers."

"Leighton did most of the work."

"He said the same thing when I saw him earlier."

"That he did most of the work?"

"No, that *you* did most of the work. You have to be patient with him, okay? He's been through hell and for every two steps forward, he'll take one step back."

Danielle snorted. "Are you changing the subject?"

"Nope, just making sure I don't leave this room with you grumbling about me." Vixen looked over her shoulder and winked. "Let me know if you need anything."

"Coffee would be nice."

Danielle bent over her keyboard and got to work. Before she did anything else, she needed to come up with a way to hide their piggy-backing. It wouldn't matter that she could pull the information from the feeds if they were discovered.

Danielle didn't know how many hours later she pushed away from her computer monitors and headed to the kitchen since a cup of coffee had never appeared on her desk. Coffee was a required food group for anyone who spent long hours bent over a keyboard putting together lines of letters and numbers defining if-then rules.

As soon as she emerged from the computer room, Foster, hopping from foot to foot in some odd game of his own creation, greeted her.

"Are you done? Vivi said I couldn't bother you until you were done. So are you done?" Foster pivoted on his left foot, spinning in rapid circles.

As cute as the kid was, his unadulterated enthusiasm overwhelmed even the most stoic of individuals after a half an hour with him. She didn't know how Finley did it. Danielle almost stepped back in with her computers, but the need for coffee outweighed the need to avoid the peppering of questions from Foster she would face on her way to the kitchen.

"Not done. Taking a break." She headed along the slight incline toward the kitchen. No matter how much her brain grasped that the house was built at an incline and into the mountain, her body always had to adjust to the slopes of the hallways from the level floors of the rooms.

"Why?" Foster hopped in a circle around her legs.

"Because I have a big project, but need to take a rest now and again."

Foster considered her words as they stepped into the kitchen. "Okay."

Just like that her answer satisfied Foster. Danielle wished everyone who asked her questions was as accepting of her responses.

Three members of the pack hovered around a space at the counter and looked over their shoulders at the newcomers. Their shoulders fell as one in relief at discovering Danielle and Foster.

"I'll play with Hampstead for you so you don't have to take as many breaks." The little boy ran off before Danielle could stop him.

"I'll make sure nothing bad happens." Finley trotted down the hallway, chasing after Foster.

"What are you all looking at?" Danielle headed toward the coffee maker on the counter.

Tevin and Allard grinned at her as they stood in front of the counter, blocking her view with their bodies.

Allard crossed his arms over his chest and stared down his nose at Danielle. "What did you promise Vixen to get her to make a Costco run just for you?"

"Huh?

Tevin stepped away and sitting on the surface, taking up nearly half of the counter space, was a giant machine made of gleaming chrome not yet marred by fingerprints. The machine had only two tasks: brew shots of espresso and steam milk.

Vixen bought Danielle an espresso maker.

And not one of the personal machines either. This one was professional and could have been found in just about any restaurant or coffee shop in the Beltway.

Danielle stepped closer to the glorious machine. A few specially brewed drinks at the right time and she wouldn't have to sleep. If she timed it right, so drink breaks coincided with bathroom breaks, Danielle could finish the so-called top-secret project assigned to her by Vixen and the General in record time. She had a strong suspicion that everyone, except Foster, knew she was working on something that involved shifters and protecting them.

Tevin spun back to face the machine and stretched an arm out to stop her from getting too close.

"Come on, don't be an ass, Tevin." Even Danielle cringed at the whiny sound of her voice.

"Shh. Just appreciate it."

"Appreciate what? Because the only thing I want to appreciate is the sweet nectar that comes out of it."

"The quiet. Bray, Leighton, and Jackson are working some magic with the pipes, so we don't have to keep the reservoir filled."

"And Vixen and Eleanor are supervising because Eleanor is convinced they'll blow up the mountain if they aren't careful."

"To be fair, Vixen is supervising because blowing up the mountain seemed sort of fun."

"Well, they'd be done with it by now, if Leighton hadn't insisted on adding a filter."

Allard and Tevin continued their conversation about exploding plumbing, but Danielle ignored them. She looked over at the massive clock on the wall that was probably a hold-over from the days before cell phones became commonplace.

It was after nine o'clock at night.

She'd been working for over six hours!

No one bothered her for dinner?

And what was Foster still doing awake?

Stupid question. With Eleanor and Jackson both preoccupied, bedtime hadn't been brought up by the others and Foster was smart enough not to draw attention to the time.

The better question was how had Vixen kept Leighton distracted for the entire afternoon and most of the evening?

Tevin slowly grinned at Danielle, as if he could read her mind. As much as Leighton said shifters didn't have any special abilities to see into her thoughts, it was moments like this that made Danielle think Leighton wasn't telling her the whole truth.

"What are you grinning at?"

"You."

"I didn't ask who, I asked what."

"Yeah, but you used the word at, implying I was grinning at something or someone, not about."

Allard smacked the back of his hand hard against Tevin's shoulder. "Don't let Vixen hear you giving Danielle shit, or we'll all be doing exercises to burn out our extra energy."

Tevin rolled his eyes and rubbed his shoulder. "The reason they're risking blowing up the mountain to get filtered water into this contraption Vixen bought, is Leighton. And the reason Vixen even bought this contraption for you is because of Leighton."

"So why the grin?"

"If his wolf, the animal that's the most broken of us all, can pick someone who isn't a serial killer, there's hope for the rest of us."

"Serial killer? Why would he… never mind. I don't want to know."

Both Allard and Tevin tilted their heads to the side and gave her one of those looks that let her know they knew she knew exactly who they were talking about. Vixen, and most everyone in Unit D, hit all the criteria of a serial killer. "Eleanor seems normal."

"We're pretty sure if Foster never surfaced, Jackson would have totally bonded with the first psycho killer who stumbled into the territory." Tevin didn't mince words. "Plus, Leighton bonded super-fast. Like faster than any of us thought poss–"

Allard reached out and smacked Tevin's shoulder again.

Danielle closed her eyes and let out a long breath while counting to five. "Explain."

"Just that bonding usually happens fast, but in his case, it was closer to instant."

Danielle slowly opened her eyes.

Shit.

She had done all that research on Leighton when Vixen first arrived at Broken Peak. What if Leighton's wolf sensed her research, and this bond wasn't a bond at all, just the wolf recognizing someone who knew enough to piece together Leighton's secrets without him having to reveal them all?

Crap on a cracker. She needed to find Leighton.

Danielle had a lot of explaining to do. And for better or worse, she needed to give Leighton the chance to walk away if his wolf picking her had nothing to do with a mating bond. "Where are they?"

"Underground tunnels." Tevin continued rubbing his shoulder and glowering at Allard. "Why?"

She spun on her heel and jogged up the hallway to the front door without answering. She had no idea where the underground tunnels were, but she figured they'd have access to the outside.

"Hey, wait up." Allard loped up behind her and grabbed her arm. "I'm not sure what lit a fire under your ass, but I don't want to know the details. Come on, I'll take you to them. If something happened to you, Leighton, Vixen, and Bray would skin me then turn me into a rug."

"Ew. That's a gross thought." She let Allard pull her back to the kitchen.

"You don't think Vixen hasn't done worse?"

"Oh, I know she has, but never to friends." She stumbled along behind Allard as he led her to a trap door in the pantry.

Allard jumped down the hole and yelled up, "come on, I'll catch you."

"I'll just stay here, guarding the espresso maker." Tevin called from the kitchen counter as Danielle dropped through the hole in the floor.

CHAPTER EIGHTEEN

BRAY, Leighton, and Jackson huddled around a group of pipes that branched off of the water main from the well, grumbling and arguing about where things went and how to best place those things. Both Eleanor and Vixen stood behind the males, rolling their eyes and wearing matching expressions of exasperation.

Danielle almost turned around. Facing Leighton on his own was scary enough, but facing him with the knowledge that the most influential members of the pack would be aware an important conversation was taking place, sent her into a near panic. She should have thought about what would happen after Allard led her through the tunnel system before she jumped down the trapdoor.

"What's wrong?" Leighton lifted his head and sniffed at the air. He wasn't looking at Danielle when he asked his question, he was staring at Allard.

"Nothing." Allard raised his hands and arms in the air in surrender. "Well, I'm sure something's wrong, Finley is supervising Foster while he plays with Hampstead, but I just brought Danielle because you'd kill me if I let her wander down here on her own."

Leighton shrugged off Allard's explanation. He wasn't wrong.

"Wait, what? Foster and Finley and Hampstead? Oh, shit!" Eleanor took off at a sprint down the darkened tunnel that would eventually emerge out to the pantry. Her shouts carried down the shaft with a small echo. "Jackson, don't blow yourself up! And Danielle, if I don't get there in time, I'm sorry and we'll replace Hampstead. I swear!"

Danielle glanced over at Vixen. "Replace?"

"It's a fifty-fifty shot that Foster will get excited and might shift then eat Hampstead. He'll feel guilty after the fact, but so far we haven't figured out a way to keep his wolf from swallowing whatever's in his mouth."

Jackson closed his eyes and bent his head forward as though in prayer. "It's a struggle."

"Once he loses his puppy teeth, it will be better." Bray spoke between chuckles and held out his hand palm up. "Now, hand me a wrench."

Danielle pressed her fingertips against her forehead and stared at her shoes. "Just tell me you haven't had to replace Hampstead already."

When no one immediately answered, Danielle looked up to find everyone looking anywhere but at her. "What? Are you serious? You've replaced Hampstead!"

Vixen held up a placating hand while the males scrunched their shoulders up to protect their hearing from Danielle's high-pitched cry.

"No, we haven't replaced him. The Hampstead in the cage is the same Hampstead that Leighton brought back. But we might have sourced potential suppliers of Hampstead lookalikes."

"I'm a grown-ass woman, don't you think I'd be okay if Hampstead had an unfortunate meeting with Foster?"

"We were thinking more of using them as decoys for Foster." Jackson had the decency to appear embarrassed by his confession.

Danielle opened her mouth, but words didn't come out right away. She had no clue where to begin and quickly gave up finding a grownup response. "At some point we're going to discuss the many layers of wrongness about this conversation, but I'm not sure that's possible without Eleanor."

"It was her idea." Bray returned his attention to the pipes. "Still waiting on the wrench."

Allard stepped around Danielle, took the wrench from Leighton's hand, and dropped the tool onto Bray's open palm. On the way, Allard shoved Leighton towards Danielle.

"Is everything okay?" Leighton picked up Danielle's hand and pulled her along the tunnel back toward the kitchen and away from the prying eyes and ears of the others.

"I don't know. I can't grasp Eleanor as the mastermind for coming up with the decoy plan for Hampstead. That's like Vixen levels of almost evil, but not quite in a narrowly defined context and completely evil in all other contexts. If Eleanor even has the slightest potential to achieve Vixen levels of evil, I was totally wrong. We have no worries about retribution for Vixen's response to the wet teams who've attacked." The words spilled from Danielle's mouth almost as quickly as they formed in her mind. "Those two women working together could redefine the definition of Axis of Evil!"

She was babbling again.

"Three."

"Huh?"

"Three. You're working on Vixen's plans, right? You'll keep them on the Axis of Good."

Danielle wasn't so sure Leighton would feel the same after she confessed the reason for running through the tunnels to find him.

At the trapdoor, Leighton grabbed Danielle by her hips and hoisted her over his head and through the opening. She scrambled over the edge and moved away from the lip. By the time she turned around to offer him a hand, he was already pulling himself up.

His muscles flexed beneath the tight fabric of his shirt. The sight almost distracted Danielle enough for her to forget what she had wanted to say.

He prowled across the pantry to the door and peered into the kitchen. When he didn't find any of his packmates there, he closed the door. Leighton dug his hands in his pockets, lowered his chin to his chest, and looked up at her with his steady gaze. "Now, tell me what's wrong?"

"Who says anything's wrong?"

"Dani…" Leighton growled out her name and the butterflies in her belly took flight.

She couldn't withstand his stare for long. "Fine. What if this bond isn't real? What if your wolf isn't pushing a bond as much as maybe he's sensing something else?"

"I have no clue what you're talking about, Dani. You need to give me more."

"I researched you. When you guys found Vixen. Well, before you found Vixen. The General gave me a head's up. But when I first did research, I didn't know about the whole shifter thing. And once I learned you were shifters, I looked into you guys a lot more. Well, more you and less the others."

Leighton's forehead crinkled as his eyebrows dropped and he stared at her with an unwavering accuracy. How did he do that? Had he been taking lessons from Vixen?

"Explain, Dani."

"I researched you. Only you. Not the pack. Like deep dive research. And both Tevin and Allard said the bond hit super-fast, like faster than normal fast, and that got me wondering. What if your wolf didn't bond with me, what if he just recognized that I know more about you than I should, unless I was a stalker. Which I'm not. Or at least I hope I'm not. A stalker, I mean. I never got to stalker levels. I might have taken a file home once or twice, but I didn't hang them in a hidden room behind a wall in the closet."

Leighton pulled his hands from his pockets, crossed his arms over his chest, and leaned back on his heels.

She was babbling again. Danielle really had to learn when to shut up. Maybe she should practice what she was going to say before she stood in front of someone and had the equivalency of diarrhea of the mouth.

"You believe, after everything that's happened, that whatever my wolf is telling me is a lie?"

"Well..." She hadn't thought about it that way. Her way made complete sense earlier, but his words made even more sense. Even if she knew his words were true, the same way she knew Vixen and the pack would keep her safe no matter what, she still couldn't shake the lingering fragment of doubt. "Humans don't have that bond thing, how am I supposed to know what it's like or if something external can cause it and make it not real?"

Leighton dropped his arms and took a step closer to her. "Don't say that. Don't ever say that what my wolf or I feel isn't real."

"But how can you say you're sure it's real? Especially after what I told you? I looked into your history, Leighton. All of those hospital visits and that your father was an asshole. I know he beat you. And it wasn't mine to look into."

He took another step closer to her. "Why did you look into me, Dani?"

"What?"

"Why did you look into me, Dani, and not the others?"

What kind of question was that? And why wasn't he pissed. If the roles had been reversed and Danielle learned Leighton knew more about her than she had shared, she'd have been... What would she have been?

Anyone else, and Danielle would have been pissed. But if Leighton dug into her past... The corners of her mouth lifted and Leighton's eyebrows raised in response.

"Find your answer?"

Danielle shook her head from side to side, but she did have the answer to his question. It wasn't concrete, and it didn't make much sense in the scheme of things, but she had an answer. "That picture from Halloween. After I saw it, I needed to learn more about you."

"Why me, Dani?"

"I'm not sure."

"Yes, you are."

"I'm not."

"You know why, Dani. The same way Eleanor and Vixen knew. The same way Bray and Jackson knew." He took another step until they stood toe to toe and pressed his hand against her cheek. "The same way *I* knew."

Danielle pulled her bottom lip between her teeth and leaned into his touch. "But..."

"But what, Dani?"

"Love isn't supposed to work that way?"

"How do you know how love works or doesn't work?" Leighton bent his head forward and pressed his lips against the top of her head.

"I don't know, but I don't think you can fall in love with a picture.

"I might not understand love like humans, but I know how bonds work. A bond between mates is stronger than any human emotion. It's permanent and ties the two together so completely that if a bond breaks, so does the shifter. What I feel for you, what my wolf feels for you, is a mating bond. My wolf had no idea what you knew about me before I saw you walking down the trail in those heels of yours. And when he saw you, everything changed. What I feel for you is more than real, Dani. It's a true bond, like the one Vixen and Bray have."

Danielle tilted her head back and blinked away her tears. Leighton never said much, but the one time he delivered a speech, it was perfect.

"What's wrong?" Leighton brushed his thumb across her cheek.

She pursed her lips and sniffed. "You aren't supposed to be the wise one. I figured I was going to be the one dragging you along, but it's the other way around."

"Maybe I've learned to listen to my wolf more than you've learned to listen to your feelings." Leighton wrapped his arms around her and pulled her up against his chest. Taking a deep breath, he nuzzled his lips against her neck and ear and cheeks. "I'm still going to fuck up though and say the wrong things. A lot."

Danielle clung to him and buried her face in his chest, taking in all of his scents and absorbing all the noises of contentment coming from both Leighton and his wolf.

She needed to make sure she kept Leighton safe. The pack safe. And if that meant building a network to intercept any communications, she'd do it. No matter what.

CHAPTER NINETEEN

A foreboding sense of urgency haunted Danielle's thoughts. Unit D wasn't letting up. Or more likely, the dickface, who Unit D served while still working for the Company. was a bigger idiot than everyone thought possible.

The alarm system she set up the week before had given them enough of a warning to intercept the teams before they got too deep into pack territory, but it was only a matter of time before Unit D changed its tech and the alarm system became obsolete. The feeds would soon be the only way to get advanced notice of any incursions. And from the gear the teams were coming in with, Unit D wasn't planning on taking any prisoners. In fact, their approach now turned into capturing Foster no matter the costs. And what happened if they couldn't get Foster? Would they find another shifter? One without the protection of Vixen and Broken Peak Pack? That's what Danielle would recommend.

Even worse, she was alone with her depressing thoughts. Danielle couldn't share why she thought Foster was the target. Not with Eleanor or Jackson or the rest of the pack. Not even Leighton. That last one was killing her a little bit. Keeping her secret caused her conscience to inflict horrid levels of guilt previously thought unimaginable. But until she had a better safety net in place in case Vixen started a war, Danielle wouldn't share the Company's plan and be the cause of a worry that wouldn't be eased with comforting words. There was a chance Vixen wouldn't antagonize the higher power if she knew Danielle's project would work.

The current struggle Danielle faced was capturing data from the feeds without setting off any alarms while her program siphoned off the data. She also needed a way to separate shifter stuff from non-shifter stuff.

Her projected time frame fluctuated depending on the size of the pit in her stomach. The larger the pit, and consequently the more coffee she needed but couldn't get because she was unable to face anyone who might be lingering in the kitchen, the longer the project's scope. And the less convinced she was of her chances for success.

Currently, the pit in her stomach had taken on black hole sized proportions and the chance of success was on par with pigs taking to the skies.

"Shit, shit, shit, shit, shit!" Her palms came down hard on her desk and the empty mug that hadn't held any coffee since hours earlier vibrated against the laminated surface.

Her head fell back, and she stared up at the rough-hewn rafters keeping the mountain from collapsing on her head. Maybe that would be how it all ended. But instead of a mountain, a pile of data would crash down on her brain, causing it to overload and turn her into a gibbering idiot.

She might not be able to face the prospect of seeing anyone in the kitchen, but she couldn't go on alone. Danielle needed help, but she needed someone who wouldn't go running back to the rest of the pack with her conundrum.

Hmm, that was interesting. The rest of the pack? Since when did she consider herself part of the pack?

"Get your mind back in the game, girl. Lollygagging about the when and why of packdom isn't helping anyone." Danielle closed her eyes and shook her head.

"Argh!" She did her best impression of Charlie Brown missing the football and pushed away from the desk. It was time to pull up her big-girl pants and face the peanut gallery in the kitchen. "Suck it up and stick on one of those grins the General told you to wear when Vixen's retirement order came through."

Great. She was talking to herself now.

None of the males would be of much help and Vixen was a definite no-go, but maybe she could recruit Eleanor without revealing too much. She heaved her body up off her chair and pushed through the door before she lost what little bravery she managed to gather around her.

"Hey, Danielle." Eleanor looked up from the table where she was helping Foster with his sight words and grinned. "Taking a break?"

Speak of the devil.

Danielle grinned right back. Except she was pretty sure her grin was more grotesque than genuine. She approached the espresso maker and used her need for a jolt of caffeine to keep her back to Eleanor. At least she wouldn't have to maintain the forced grin.

"I wish. A break means I actually did work." Danielle pushed the buttons in their proper order and waited for the espresso to brew.

She turned and leaned back against the counter while watching Eleanor walk Foster through the process of recognizing the word "could" by the silent letter "l". A concept that annoyed Foster if the glare he sent the flash card's way was anything to go by.

"We'll just set this one aside for later." Eleanor set "could" on the table face down so it wouldn't taunt Foster while he worked on his other words.

"So, are you the only one who does school stuff with Foster or does Jackson work with him too?" It wouldn't be fair to ask Eleanor to help if she was the only one who handled Foster's schooling.

"Jackson?" Eleanor snorted and rolled her eyes. "God no. We decided early on he would handle the wolf things and I would handle the not-fun things. Although, Finley is surprisingly good with the not-fun things."

"Think he might be willing to help out for a few days? I'm at a bit of a loss and Vixen mentioned some of your research included a lexicon."

"We can ask him." Eleanor held up a card with the word "again" printed in large block letters across the front.

Foster glowered at the card. "Again, but it should be a gain."

"Remember when I said that we need to ignore all the rules because there are exceptions? These words are all exceptions."

"Well that's stupid." Foster crossed his arms over his chest.

"What do you say we find Finley now?" Eleanor looked over at Danielle and delivered a tight smile. "Think we'll have to bribe him?"

"Or just have Vixen ask him." Danielle shrugged and turned back to her coffee. "Wanna cup?"

"Only if it comes with a shot of bourbon." Eleanor turned back to Foster. "Do Mommy a favor?"

Foster closed an eye and studied his mother, considering all the potential tasks Eleanor might come up with before agreeing to the unknown favor. "Maybe."

"Go find Uncle Finley and bring him here, please." Eleanor swept up the flash cards into a neat stack.

"Okay, Mommy." Foster scampered away from the table, happy to be away from the flash cards.

With her son sent safely off on a task and not likely to be back soon, Eleanor focused her full attention on Danielle. "I'm not sure I understand your project or why Vixen is so impatient to see it completed, but from what I've overheard you're looking for words specific to the shifter community?"

Danielle finished making her coffee and sipped the steaming hot ambrosia before answering. "Actually, I need words unique to the shifter community."

"I don't think there are any. It's not like they have their own language. They don't need to use coded words since they can tell if someone's a shifter or not." Eleanor leaned back in the chair and stared across the kitchen in thought.

Not wanting to interrupt Eleanor's muse, Danielle busied herself with making another latte.

Foster returned with Finley in tow before the second coffee finished. As soon as the boy walked into the kitchen, he returned to the chair next to his mother and resumed his reluctant posture regarding the flash cards. The kid really hated the concept of sight words. Eleanor and Jackson must have used bribery to convince him he had to memorize the words on the cards.

No matter how complex or impossible the task Vixen sent Danielle's way, she'd prefer it to homeschooling Foster.

"You need some mommy time?" The young male shifter looked between the two women, shoved his hands in his pockets, and leaned back on his heels. "It's gonna cost you."

Eleanor narrowed her eyes at Finley. "Vixen needs me to help Danielle. Send Vixen the bill."

Damn, Eleanor was good at getting the pack to do what she needed. Danielle made a mental note to use the Vixen card more often.

"Fine." Finley let out a long and loud sigh, but approached the table with a wary look at Foster. "What do you need me to do?"

"He has to memorize these words, so he knows them on sight." Eleanor gestured to the stack of green cards. "The ones with blue stickers are the words he knows, the red ones are the ones we're still working on. Our goal is to put a blue sticker on another card today."

Finley grumbled something about losing his favorite uncle status if he wasn't careful, but sat down next to Finley and grabbed the stack of flash cards. "Okay, kid, looks like it's you and me and cookies when you get a blue sticker."

"Come on, we have two hours, three if we're lucky. But in three hours we'll have to pause for dinner." Eleanor sped out of the kitchen and down the hallway towards her room. "I have some old journals that might help."

Danielle raced after her with both cups of coffee in hand. For the first time in days, the pit in her stomach faded away. She didn't know how she was going to do it yet, but Danielle was determined her program wouldn't only keep Broken Peak Pack safe, but every shifter.

CHAPTER TWENTY

THE government had been sending in two-man teams every few days for the past few weeks. If not for Dani's alarm system going off whenever anyone got too close, the pack would be running ragged keeping their territory secure.

The Company casualties were adding up, but the lost men didn't slow the frequency of the incursions. Just the day before, Vixen and Leighton interrogated one of the men and learned Dani had replaced Vixen as Enemy Number One. The revelation sent Leighton and his wolf into full-blown protector mode and it was all Vixen could do to stop Leighton from killing their prisoner before extracting more information.

Which was a good thing, because they also learned the teams didn't know the shifters used technology to track the invaders. Instead, the Company believed the shifters of Broken Peak relied on their heightened sense of smell. No one had a clue about the alarm system.

Sure, Leighton and the other wolf shifters could scent out intruders, but not at the same distance of the receivers. Thankfully, their enemy didn't have enough information about shifters and Vixen planned on keeping it that way.

After Leighton's loss of control, Vixen gave him the day off. And for the first time in forever, Leighton and his packmates felt secure enough to step outside and let their wolves run when they weren't on patrol. Well, except for Dani. No way in hell was Leighton going to let her step one foot off the porch without the entire pack, plus Roose and Gareth and Gareth's entire clan patrolling the forest.

Leighton planned on letting his wolf run, but it was nearing the end of November and almost colder than a well-digger's ass. Plus, Foster needed a break from the tedium of being stuck inside the Lodge. So Leighton volunteered to watch the pup play in the yard. Eleanor relented when Jackson intervened and suggested that they either let Foster run in the yard or implement the "Hampstead Decoy" plan.

Leighton leaned back on the porch swing and used his foot to move it back and forth. Unfortunately, Dani was working hard on her project and couldn't join him during his babysitting duty. Leighton might be able to drag Dani to dinner and bed, but she rarely left her bank of computers for a much needed breath of fresh air. Dani claimed it was because she was close to finishing and didn't want to stop her momentum. On the plus side, she promised to text him when she was ready for a break.

That was another thing the pack needed to thank Dani for. She supplied everyone in the pack and their allies with encrypted cell phones. Even Foster got one, a heavily modified phone with limited contacts. Not like Foster would call anyone, the phone was more so the pack could locate the pup in an emergency. She swore up and down the phones were secure and safe to use as long as they only used them to communicate with each other and didn't call anyone not on their contact lists.

Leighton's wolf, and Leighton too if he was being honest, loved having another way to keep tabs on Dani with the phone. He had to remind his wolf that she wouldn't appreciate him camping out in her computer room when he wasn't on guard duty. The phone was a bit of a compromise and kept his wolf from planting his ass in front of the door and shadowing her on the way to the kitchen for her coffee breaks. The only problem, as far as Leighton was concerned, was that Dani didn't always reply as quickly as he liked. Which was why he almost fell out of the swing to dig his phone out of his pocket when it vibrated. He expected a text, but when he looked down at the screen, there wasn't a text notification. She was calling him.

He brushed his thumb against the fingerprint scanner to unlock the phone and lifted it to his ear while monitoring the pup as he pounced on what appeared to be a field mouse. At least it wasn't a frog.

"Hey there, need coffee, food, or a break?" He answered the phone with a hopeful question.

"Where are you?"

"Outside watching Foster's wolf attack a mouse. You didn't answer me."

"Grab him and come down to Mission Control. Grab the others too."

"What? Really?" Leighton pushed up to his feet and moved the phone away from his mouth to whistle at the pup. "You're inviting us into your den? Why?"

Foster lifted his head toward Leighton and the porch before swallowing whatever he had caught then trotted back to the lodge. Bringing the pup into the Lodge wasn't ideal, but waiting for Foster to shift back would take too much time.

"I want you all to witness going live with the project I've been working on."

"You're done already? I thought you were weeks away from finishing." Leighton's heart raced at the thought of Dani spending more time with him. Sure, she'd still spend hours at her computers, but Leighton would have a better chance of pulling her away for occasional breaks.

"The hardest part was figuring out how to make it work. Once I found a solution, typing on the keyboard was the easy part."

"Shit. That was fast." Leighton opened the front door and corralled the young wolf inside. "Is there a time limit or something?"

"Time limit?" Dani's confusion made itself known by the way she dragged out the word limit at a high-pitch.

"Do I have more than five minutes to get everyone to your computer room?" Leighton bent down and picked up Foster by the nape of his neck. The last thing the pack needed was a wolf pup running around underfoot.

"What? Yeah. I can go live whenever I want. It's not like the program has a mind of its own."

"Okay, I'll get everyone there." Leighton pressed the phone between his ear and shoulder while he secured the limp pup under his free arm. "Can't wait to spend time with you before dinner, Dani."

Dani fell silent on the other end of the phone and Leighton worried he might have incorrectly assumed she'd have more time for him with the project finally finished.

"Leighton?" She uttered a nervous whisper.

"Yeah?" Leighton wasn't sure he wanted to hear what she had to say. When Dani got nervous, it usually meant her mind went off on a tangent that didn't bode well for him.

"I want you to know I love you."

"Both me and my wolf love you too, Dani." Leighton stopped mid-stride and tightened his arm around the wriggling puppy. Dani was big on feelings, but she rarely made random declarations of love. "Hey, what's going on?"

"Nothing. It's just…" She hesitated and Leighton almost dropped Foster to race down the hallway to her. "I just wanted you to know. Now hurry and get everyone down here, while I let you go, so I can make sure everything will work."

She ended the call before Leighton responded.

Shit. That didn't sound good. What the hell had Vixen convinced Dani to do to get her to tell Leighton she loved him?

He stood in the hallway with a squirming pup who attacked his neck and ear with licks.

Hearing his woman saying she loved him made his day great. However, if he thought too long about the reason she said the words, the day might lose its shine.

Double shit.

"Come on, pup, let's go find your mom and the others." Leighton continued walking down the hallway and called for the rest of the pack to meet him at the computer room. Eleanor and General Jesup wouldn't hear him unless they were close by, but Jackson and Vixen would make sure they came along.

He stopped at the kitchen and handed Foster off to Jackson.

"What's going on?" Finley asked as he met them just outside the kitchen.

"Not sure exactly, but Dani said she finished the project and wants us to see it go live. Whatever that means."

Vixen, Bray, and Allard joined them. It was turning into a regular party.

"She did? Bray, call Mac and tell him to get his ass over here. Allard, find the General and bring him down to the computer room." Vixen rubbed her hands together and bounced up and down on the balls of her feet. "I can't believe she did it. The General and I told her she could do it, but honestly, I wasn't sure it was possible."

"What exactly did you ask her to do?" Leighton asked.

"Just the impossible. And if it works, it'll be a game changer. Hell, if it works, I'll have you guys install the espresso machine in her computer room." Vixen pushed through the group of males and led the way towards the room Dani had been hiding out in since she arrived at Broken Peak.

Leighton had a love hate relationship with that room. It brought Dani to him, but it also kept her from spending time with him.

Finley peeled off from the group and headed to the pantry.

"Where are you going?" Jackson shifted Foster from one arm to the other, stopping the pup's exuberant attempts to clean whatever crumbs he could find in Jackson's whiskers.

"We don't have any champagne, but I think there are a few jugs of Mac's moonshine left." Finley grinned over his shoulder. "No clue what this is all about, but it sounds like a good enough reason for a celebratory drink."

Jackson turned to his mate, prepared to hand off Foster, but Eleanor held up her hands and stepped back. "No way. He's too heavy for me to do more than lift him off the bed. I'll grab cups and food. We should have something in our stomachs if we're going to drink that stuff."

She followed Finley into the kitchen and just as quickly as almost all the pack had gathered in the hallway, they broke off to complete their tasks.

Knowing Dani, she'd be peeking out the door on the lookout for them and Leighton didn't want to keep her waiting. Dani had little patience when it came to things that didn't involve her computer. He shouldered past the others and sped walked down the hallway. He even got his arms and hips swinging in that weird motion when Tevin caught up with him and elbowed Leighton into the wall.

Leighton retaliated with a well-placed shoulder, "scrote."

"Lamer," Tevin responded by running into Leighton.

"Peckerwood." Leighton palmed the top of Tevin's head, but it didn't slow him down.

"Clodpole."

"Dingleberry."

Leighton kept walking as Tevin alternated between bouncing against the wall and Leighton as they made their way towards Dani.

Vixen grumbled something about making them all go for a run along the border before dinner, but she didn't need to worry. As soon as Dani's grin greeted Leighton and she wiggled her fingers at him, Tevin could have come after Leighton with a chainsaw and Leighton would have ignored his younger packmate.

"I can't believe I'm nervous for this." Vixen rolled her eyes and spoke to no one in particular.

"Why?" Jackson shifted Foster to his other side.

"Because if this works the way we hope it will, everything will change. We're witnessing history being made."

Eleanor caught up to the group with an armful of snacks. "Danielle used my research and journals. Does that mean I get credit for helping?"

"Come on, just tell us what it is so we don't have to hover around and pretend like we understand it and are as excited as you." Finley grumbled from the back of the group.

Bray reached behind and gave the back of Finley's head a smack. "Jackson will agree. It's just easier this way."

Dani's eyes grew big as plates as the pack drew closer and backed into the room. "I guess I forgot how many there are of you. I'm not sure you'll all fit." She sat down in front of the computer. "Is Mac here?"

"I'm here." The old curmudgeon slipped in.

"Chances are, I'll need you a lot in the beginning. Until we get all the algos narrowed down."

Leighton growled low and crossed his arms over his chest. Why didn't Dani need him? Why'd she need an old male who was well past his expiration date?

Dani's fingers flew across the keyboard. "Maybe I should have thought this through. You might end up seeing a pile of gibberish."

Finley leaned closer and stared at the dark computer screen glowing with green letters and numbers. "Hate to break it to you, but I'm looking at gibberish right now."

Dani cocked her head to the side and stared at the screen for a moment before releasing a soft giggle. "I don't expect you to understand what's on this screen, it's what comes across the other screen that matters." She waved her hand in front of the blank computer screen like Vanna White waving at the board holding the hidden letters.

"What are we supposed to be looking at?" Tevin asked the question everyone in the room wanted to ask, but was too afraid of asking in case they were the only ones who didn't know.

"Nothing yet." Dani's fingers returned to their fluid movement over the keyboard, as she pulled her bottom lip between her teeth. "But in about forty-five seconds you will."

As if on command, lines of words appeared on the blank screen. Everyone standing crab walked two steps to the left and bent forward to peer at the monitor.

Bray squinted and pushed his way closer to the screen.

"Bray, why don't you just surrender to aging and get a pair of glasses already?"

He grunted, then threw his arm around Vixen's shoulder and pulled her close against his side. "That would take away the pleasure of you telling me what I'm supposed to be seeing."

Eleanor and Vixen shared a look. Similar to the looks the women shared with their mates when they didn't need words to convey their feelings. Leighton wondered if he and Dani would ever share those looks with each other before realizing it didn't matter. Shared looks wouldn't make him love her more than he already did.

Leighton stepped back as the realization rolled over him. Was this what his father felt for his mother? Another step back until the wall pressed against his shoulders, stopping his retreat.

Vixen, with her apparent second sense, glanced over her shoulder at him and lifted her chin. Her knowing grin and slight shake of her head was enough to stop Leighton from sidestepping to the door and backing out of the room. He didn't think her griffin was capable of reading minds, but he wouldn't put it past her. Her understanding slowed his pounding heart, and he returned his attention to what was happening inside the room instead of inside himself.

Letters and numbers scrolled across the screen. Names and what looked like phone numbers. None of them recognizable.

"It's just a name, Danielle."

"Yep. But it's tied to a phone number. My program listens in and pulls out numbers that match specific criteria. It's searching for a pattern. In this case," Dani turned her gaze away from her screen with lines of code to the screen the others were staring at, "the pattern is centered around a number belonging to a Maggie Iotor. Either she's at risk as a shifter or will cause harm to shifters."

"Uh, Danielle..." Vixen cleared her throat.

"Nope. That's all we're getting. I'm not allowing a program to determine intent. That's for humans, er shifters, to decide."

Mac cleared his throat, "I spent hours with her on this. Shifters can and do cause harm to other shifters, if we assumed only government on shifter harm, we'll be missing the bigger picture of this project."

"Is that area code in West Virginia?"

"Yeah, for now the program has a narrow scope. Over time, it will widen, but I need to train it how to recognize patterns. If it pulled a number from California, we might waste a lot of time traveling there only to discover the program misunderstood the data."

Bray pressed his fingertip against the screen. "What does this number mean?"

Everyone peered at his finger. 427.

Dani glanced over and cocked her head to the side. "Touches. The program found 427 individual contacts to her number that fit inside the pattern."

"Four hundred and twenty seven calls since you pushed the on button for your program?" Someone asked in disbelief of the size of the number.

"Four hundred and twenty-seven times someone or ones referred to her number." Dani's voice lowered, and she slid her chair over to the screen, pushing the others away. "Since we had access to the feeds..."

"That's been what? Three days?" Vixen pushed Bray and the others behind her. "How many calls."

"In or out?" Dani asked.

"Both."

"None in and one out. To a..." Dani typed away at her keyboard, "hotel. Not a very nice one from the looks of it either."

Vixen reached down and squeezed Dani's shoulder while the rest of the pack looked at each other. If their expressions of confusion were anything to go by, they were all as lost as Leighton. Something important was going on, but it was beyond anyone's experience to understand the quick back and forth between Vixen and Dani.

Leighton decided right then and there he would learn everything about Dani's program so he could have the same connection with her that Vixen had.

"Finley and Tevin?" Vixen stretched her arm behind her and snapped her fingers.

"Yeah, Vixen?"

Jackson handed Foster to Eleanor and her knees nearly buckled from the weight of the pup. But like the wolves in the room, Eleanor realized something heavy was about to go down and didn't complain about the burden.

"Get to the garage. We'll give you your destination once you're on the road, but looks like you're heading to War." Vixen didn't bother looking at them and kept her gaze locked on the screen. "And gear up. Fully loaded with the body armor."

"Seriously?" Tevin scratched the back of his neck. "That shit is hot. Even if it's almost December."

"Yes." Vixen's single word response left no room for disagreement.

"I'll go with them." General Jesup declared.

"None of the numbers are government numbers." Dani responded.

"Are you certain? They could be assigned to any number of dummy corps."

"Unless the black ops teams have started using cell phone plans with popular carriers and are stupid enough to have all the numbers under one large corporate plan, I'm going to go with being certain the touches aren't government." Dani's fingers continued flying across both keyboards.

Leighton gave up attempting to decipher her actions and the conversation and instead relished in his growing pride for his woman. That was *his* mate. His mate taking control and doing whatever magic she did with her computers.

Vixen snapped her head around and glared at the pack lingering behind her. "What are you two still doing here? General, if you want to go, I wouldn't be against it. This might not be a government op, but it has all the signatures of..." Vixen trailed off as she turned her attention back to the computer screen.

"Snatch and grab." Dani supplied.

Both Eleanor and Vixen looked at Mac, but it was Eleanor who spoke up, surprising everyone. "Are you kidding me? Not only do we have to worry about the government kidnapping people, but now we need to add shifters to our list?"

Both Tevin and Finley used Eleanor's outburst to escape the room. Leighton didn't blame them. Waves of pressure rolled off Vixen and covered the remaining shifters. Foster whined and burrowed his head against Eleanor. Leighton wouldn't be surprised if the humans weren't feeling the strength of Vixen's power.

"We live off the grid and away from the prying eyes of most agencies."

"Leighton went to the hospital." Dani contradicted Mac's words.

"There are always exceptions." Mac growled in response. "Different shifters have different rules. Hell, even different packs have different customs. It's not like we have a central organization to oversee all shifters."

"Maybe we should." Vixen hissed. Her griffin was pushing her way to the surface if the noises coming from their Alpha female were anything to go by.

"Maybe we will." Eleanor concurred.

"One war at a time." Bray's hand rubbed small circles on Vixen's lower back. The gesture soothed Vixen and the pressure in the room lifted.

Leighton made a mental note. Touches eased tension. If Dani was going to be spending her time interpreting messages on her computer screen, she'd likely be more tense than Vixen, if that was even possible. His wolf wasn't pleased with the idea of Dani having any stress and seconded Leighton's plan on using touch.

Bray kept his hand on Vixen, but turned so he could see the others in the room. "You all go on with your duties. Jackson, call Gareth and see if he's willing to give us two men to pick up Finley and Tevin's patrol. Eleanor, why don't you take Foster down to the cellar and let him explore until he shifts back."

As the others left the room, quick to obey Bray's commands, Leighton lingered in the doorway. He knew he should follow orders delivered by an Alpha, but he couldn't leave Dani alone. His wolf wouldn't let him. Bray glared at Leighton and opened his mouth, but Vixen's hand on Bray's arm and a slight shake of her head, barely noticeable, silenced him.

Leighton slipped to the corner. He wasn't smart in the same ways as Dani or Mac or even Vixen. There wasn't much he'd be able to add to their conversation, but he'd be damned if they made him leave. At a young age, Leighton learned the art of invisibility to stay safe. Now, years later, he used those same skills to keep his mate safe.

"Mac?" Vixen's question interrupted Leighton's thought.

"Yeah?"

"What am I sending the boys into?"

Mac shrugged. "Without knowing what Maggie is, I can't say."

"She's a raccoon." Dani supplied while she typed.

"How do you know? I thought you couldn't see the content of calls or messages. Wasn't that part of the deal?" Vixen lurched toward the computers, hoping to find something on the screen that gave more information than what Dani had agreed to pull.

"Nope, can't see any of that. What you're seeing on the screen is all I can see. Name, phone number, and data points the program used to determine whether to show it to us."

"Then how do you know she's a raccoon? Are there even raccoon shifters, Mac?"

"Why not? Not all shifters are apex predators. There are moose and deer shifters, and raptors too. There are badger and fox shifters, so why not raccoons?"

Dani rubbed the corner of her eyes with her middle finger and thumb. "Look at her last name."

When Bray, Mac, and Vixen stared at the screen, expecting to see something new. Leighton shuffled forward and Vixen made room for him.

With the pack finally healthy, having both a male and female Alpha, the others deferred to Jackson as the second. After all, he was the oldest, the first one mated, and also a father. The others accepted Jackson, and Bray and Vixen often pulled him inside the room where they discussed pack matters before speaking with the rest of the pack. Leighton might not have been invited into the room, but he wasn't being kicked out either. Was this weird feeling of helplessness, knowing your decision would affect the life of one or many, what leading a pack was all about? Leighton rubbed the back of his neck. As dominant as his wolf was, he should be leading a pack as an Alpha and Leighton understood that someday he'd have to leave Broken Peak and do just that. Of all the difficulties he'd considered, living with the consequences of even the smallest of decisions hadn't ever entered his thoughts.

"Iotor is the species part of the scientific name for raccoons."

Bray shook his head, jostling his thoughts together. "How did you know that?"

Dani rolled her eyes and pointed to yet another monitor. This one showed a page from Wikipedia. "I Googled it."

"Okay, so assuming she's a raccoon, what do you know about them?"

"They keep to themselves, are phenomenal thieves, and we don't want to mess with them if we can help it. They don't like outsiders and rarely let anyone leave their gazes." Leighton answered Vixen's question.

"How do you know about–"

"The touches are increasing."

Dani interrupted the question-and-answer portion of the discussion and saved Leighton from having to explain the hell of having a gaze living close to the town he grew up in. Gazes were a sick combination of a cult and a gang.

"And from what I can tell, her phone's gone dark. She might have yanked the sim card or destroyed the phone if she's worried."

"So she's not at that hotel?" Vixen asked.

"Would you be?"

"No." Vixen patted the top of Dani's head. "See if you can get confirmation on her last known location. Jesup is with the boys, so they won't be completely in the dark."

Dani slid her chair back in front of the screen with the lines of gibberish and typed madly away. "Already on it."

Vixen eyed Bray and Mac and pursed her lips in thought. "We'll need to reinforce our borders. We're about due for another incursion."

"Got it handled. I'll grab Roose and Gareth. The three of us should be able to compensate for dividing the pack." Bray said.

"Is that code for we'll discuss it later because I know better than to disagree with you in front of company?" Mac guffawed and elbowed Bray in the ribs. "Come on, I'll head out with you."

"Where are you going old man?" Vixen asked.

"No where you need to worry about." Mac left before Vixen asked any more questions.

Leighton didn't blame him one bit. Vixen was amazing at extracting what she wanted to know.

That left Leighton, Dani, and Vixen alone in the room. "If Dani's program is right, this could..."

"Change everything. I know" Dani didn't look away from her screen.

"Do you need anything? I want to check on some of our security measures, but I'll be back in a few."

"Coffee would be great." Dani still hadn't looked up from her computer screen.

"I'll get you coffee."

"No, you stay here." Vixen stepped out of the computer room and closed the door behind her.

Now that the room was empty, but for Dani and Leighton, he wasn't sure what to say.

"Hey Leighton?"

"Yeah?" He didn't know what else to do, but took a cue from Bray and pressed his hand down on Dani's shoulder.

She covered his hand with hers and squeezed. "I agreed to build this program because of you. It would have alerted on you and stopped any of the hurt and pain."

"But then Mac wouldn't have found me and brought me here." Leighton bent down and kissed the top of her head. "I used to hate my father, Dani. I still do, but not as much since you. Without him, I never would have found you and you never would have found me."

Dani turned her head and kissed the underside of his wrist. "Your wolf would have found someone else, I'm sure."

"No he wouldn't. You're it for me. You're the one. Like Jackson and Eleanor. He even had a kid with another woman, but Eleanor is it for him. And Bray was in his forties before he found Vixen." Leighton spun her chair so she couldn't avoid him by staring at her computer screens. He dropped to his knees and squeezed the tops of her legs. "You're my mate Dani Howe. I love you, and I want to claim you. Will you wear my mark? I mean, if you want."

Dani stared down at him and slow blinked. "Yes. I think. Wait. Are you proposing? Is this like getting married for shifters?"

"Yes, but more." He smiled at her. "Is that a yes?"

"It's a yes." Dani pressed her hands against his cheeks and leaned forward until her lips found his. "I love you, Leighton."

Leighton didn't stop kissing her, not even when he told her he loved her back.

TURN THE PAGE FOR *BROKEN MAGE EXTRAS,* INCLUDING

The official, Jules Crisare-Sanctioned "What Kind of Shifter are You?" Quiz

An excerpt from the next Broken Peak novel, *BROKEN REBEL*

And More!

THE OFFICIAL "WHAT KIND OF SHIFTER ARE YOU?" QUIZ

You've read Broken Hero and laughed at the antics of the Broken Peak Pack and cheered when Bray claimed Vixen and accidentally on purpose released the Griffin lurking inside of her. Right? I mean maybe you didn't do all those things, but let's just pretend you have. Now, I bet you're wondering where you'd fit in the pack. Would you be a wolf shifter? Or a griffin shifter? Or maybe another kind of shifter entirely. Well, you no longer have to wonder. In the short time it takes you to answer the questions below, you'll find out what kind of shifter you are.

WHAT SHIFTER AM I?

(If you want to find out what kind of shifter your partner is, replace "you" with "he/she/they". Depending on the result, you might want to keep it to yourself.)

1. When Vixen and Bray invite you to a barbecue at Broken Peak, you:

    a. Hide in the woods and hope no one finds you

    b. Show up earlier and be the last to leave and drink the most moonshine

2. Vixen asks you to steal a shifter artifact from a private collector who refuses to sell (there's no chance of getting caught), you:

    a. Tell her no way

    b. Tell her sure, why not

3. Vixen thinks you should find a mate, you:

    a. Go out with whoever Mac recommends, and of course they're a perfect match, so you agree.

    b. Create profiles on shifter-r-us with the rest of Broken Peak Pack and go out on group dates so your friends can give you instant advice. Plus, if they don't like your friends, they aren't for you.

4. War passed a new ordinance, barring all concealed weapons, even daggers, you:

   a. Don't bring the dagger Vixen got for you into town and leave it at home instead

   b. Ignore the ordinance, besides it's not like you go to War all that often

5. After a long day chasing down false alarms that led no where followed by a double dose of training from Vixen, you just want to go home and fall into bed, but your best friend sends a text, asking if you want to go out for dinner in thirty minutes, you:

   a. Call them back right away, since you plan on venting and your best friend is a great listener

   b. Ignore the message and call your friend back the next morning, you plan on spending the night alone with your favorite book

6. While walking through the park late at night with no one around, you see a new "Keep Off Grass" sign, you:

   a. Complain to yourself, but avoid walking on the grass

   b. Yank the sign out, throw it into the trees, then gleefully hop around on the grass since there's no more sign to stop you

ANSWERS

1. a=1, b=0

3. a=0, b=1

4. a=1, b=0

5. a=0, b=1

6. a=1, b=0

Add up your points! Have the number? Great, now if you scored:

0-1 GRIFFIN
Always up for a group hunt or hanging out with the pack, even if it means exploring forbidden territory.

2 WOLF
You take every opportunity to spend time with your friend and pack and always obey your Alpha.

3-4 COYOTE
You don't mind occasionally hanging out with friends, but prefer to spend most of your time alone with your still and never let something like rules get in the way of doing something.

5-6 BEAR
You're the strong and silent type, always ready to help your few close friends you have as long as your aren't breaking any rules.

AN EXCERPT FROM THE NEXT BROKEN PEAK PACK NOVEL, *BROKEN REBEL*

Finley doesn't want or need a mate. Broken Peak isn't safe for a female or pups. His wolf has other ideas. When a female he's never met is threatened, he's convinced the only place she's safe is at Broken Peak. Living with the Pack and him. As his mate. There's only one problem ... she needs to leave Broken Peak behind to keep the shifters who live there safe from the deranged leader of her Gaze set on bringing her back into the fold whatever cost.

So far she'd pieced together that bears, wolves, mountain lions, a coyote, a badger, and something she couldn't identify because whenever it came out, her raccoon took over, locked the woman side of her inside, and hid in the hole in her tree. Except for the not-human beastie, as far as Maggie knew, none of the kinds of shifters living in the region allied themselves to the Gazes.

Smart beasts.

Well, that was something you didn't see every day.

The pup was running right to her. And scurrying along over the brown grass in front of the pup was a tan little rodent thingy sold in human pet stores.

Maggie couldn't remember what they were called, but it didn't matter because the fat little roly poly was headed right for her.

Did it have no survival instincts whatsoever? Not that she made a meal of furry roly polys on the regular, but if they ran right into her paws? Well, who didn't appreciate a snack?

Maggie fought against her animal's instinct. Hard. Eating the roly poly wasn't smart in the scheme of things.

The roly poly wasn't stopping. Neither was the wolf pup.

Before instinct took over, Maggie pushed her animal aside and took over as much control as she could. It wasn't much, but it was enough. She darted the few feet out of the safety of the woods and grabbed the roly poly with her front paws and hugged it close to her chest while fighting all the instincts telling her to rub her paws around the roly poly.

Crapsicles.

She hadn't thought her plan through. Standing up on her back legs, she was barely the same height as the pup. The same pup who wanted what she had in her paws. The same pup who wasn't happy that he lost his prize. The same pup who latched on to the nape of her neck and was now trotting back to the house.

And the shifter standing on the porch that she just now saw as they closed the distance between the safety of the woods and the unknown of the house.

She twisted around in the pup's grip. At least he wasn't hurting her, but without releasing the roly poly, she couldn't get away.

Assuming the cabin in front of her didn't lead back to the Gaze, the roly poly was her ticket inside. She couldn't just drop it.

"Well, that's not something you see every day." The low rumbling, almost growly voice of the male caused her animal to push forward. Well, the sound of his voice *and* his scent. She'd recognize it anywhere after he left it all over her camper.

Her animal wanted, no *needed*, to see the male who spoke too.

Both animal and woman stared at the male standing at the top of a short set of stairs. Dark hair, long enough to brush the collar of his thermal shirt. Maggie's animal couldn't see what color his shirt was, but she thought it was blue or green.

Stupid animal. Maggie wanted to see him, but her animal wasn't giving up her body anytime soon.

"What did you find, Foster? A new friend?" The male asked with a soft chuckle.

Maggie's entire body shook as the wolf pup wiggled. She only just held on to the roly poly.

The male walked down the stairs with slow, careful steps and crouched down in front of all three animals. "You know better than to chase Hampstead."

The roly poly had a name. Good thing she hadn't eaten it.

The male held his hand out, palm up. "Why don't you give me Hampstead, then I'll make Foster let you go and no one risks getting squished."

Was he implying she would squish the roly poly? She hadn't taken a bite out of it yet. Besides, flattening things wasn't her style. Silly male. Maggie hissed.

Crapsicles.

Hissing was bad. Hissing always led to corrections from the enforcers in the Gaze.

She closed her eyes tight and shrunk back as much as possible while hanging from the mouth of a wolf pup.

A correction never came.

Instead, a warm laugh sent a fresh wave of tingles through her body.

Good tingles. Not the bad tingles warning her something painful was about to happen.

Maggie opened one eye.

The super sexy male was still crouched in front of her with his hand out, but he wasn't frowning or glowering. He full-on smiled at her, showing all of his perfectly straight teeth.

Maggie thought he had the nicest smile she'd ever seen. His smile was genuine, not the leering smiles of the males who worked closely with Zachery. Their smiles never reached their eyes. The smile she saw now not only reached the male's eyes, but caused funny crinkles at the corners.

"You're a spunky little thing, aren't you?"

Maggie opened her other eye and stretched her front legs out as far as they went, but she still didn't let go of the roly poly. That was her animal's doing.

Treasures were treasures, even furry ones.

The male reached behind his back. Maggie shut her eyes and pulled the roly poly back to her chest.

She had been wrong. A correction was coming.

"Hey, cutie, I have something for you. A trade."

His words didn't make sense. No one at the Gaze called her cutie or cute. They called her willful and prideful and sometimes stupid. And no one had ever offered her a trade. They just took.

She opened both eyes. The male's hand was still reaching out with the palm up, but his other hand held something shiny. Something that no one in the Gaze would ever allow her to hold on to for very long.

A pocket knife! And not one of those dinky ones either. The one he held out to her was as big as his palm.

Neither her animal nor Maggie had to think about it for long. She reached her front legs out and dropped the roly poly in the open palm, then snatched the shiny before the male could take it away.

Ha. She had a shiny!

And not just any shiny, it was a sharp shiny.

She had a *sharpy*!

She chittered happily while running her paws over the object. It was still warm. Like it had been close to the male's body. And it smelled like him. The raccoon wanted to run her nose all over it, but Maggie thought sniffing a knife might come across as weird and convinced her animal she could smell away once they were in private. The excitement over the sharpy was enough to distract her from the fact she was still hanging from the mouth of the wolf pup.

"You like it?"

Like it? She loved it. Maggie might have even been singing a silly song about her sharp shiny. She chittered back at him and hoped the male understood.

"If Foster lets you go, will you stick around?"

Whoa there. The chittering halted.

"Don't run away, okay?" The male's smile was still there. "You're safe here. I promise."

Maggie believed him. She could tell if he lied, but she didn't need that sense to know she could trust him.

She chittered. Or maybe her raccoon chittered. At this point her animal had enough control that Maggie pushing her to run away might well be impossible.

The male's smile grew even bigger. "Okay, Foster, let her go."

The wolf pup whined, but didn't let her go.

Crapsicles. Of all the possible ways this scenario could have played out, the wolf pup not letting her go hadn't crossed her mind.

"Foster, don't make me get Vivi." The male stood with an effortless grace and covered the roly poly with his free hand before the furry thing could make another escape.

Maggie didn't understand who Vivi was or why she, or it, was a threat, but Foster dropped Maggie. Which under most circumstances would have been good. Except, no way in hell was her raccoon releasing the sharpy. Maggie tottered on her hind legs and side-eyed the three steps. It wouldn't be the first time she climbed steps on her hind legs, but it hadn't been pretty those other times and it wouldn't be now.

Her raccoon had enough sense to hold on to the sharpy with one paw and keep the other paw free so when she fell, which was a strong possibility, her snout wasn't at risk of being flattened.

What an embarrassing grand entrance.

ACKNOWLEDGMENTS

SITTING DOWN TO WRITE AN acknowledgment page is much like making an acceptance speech at an award's show. It's more than likely that you will forget someone and then have to spend hours on the phone apologizing for the misstep. And God help you, if it's your mother. So, I should probably get that one out of the way first, right? I need to acknowledge my parents, especially my mother, who have supported me and define the phrase unconditional love.

The readers of the Broken Peak Pack and the Sentinels of the Silver Orb. Without them, Danielle and Leighton's story would never be told. Your enthusiasm for the series and emails in my inbox keep me writing each new story in this universe.

Love and thanks to Cassandra V. She's my cheerleader, friend, and taskmaster. The shifters of Broken Peak thrived because of her support and encouragement.

Chan, she's a pillar of unconditional support and a reminder that I am not a complete and total hack when the insecurity hits and I spiral into the dreaded impostor syndrome.

I would be remiss in not thanking my friends and family, who put up with me during my seclusion in the writing cave and constantly offer their support and love.

Finally, and of course not least, the wonderful individuals who are responsible for the creation of the collector's edition of the Broken Peak Pack Omnibus: Kasey S., Sherry M., Meg M., Pyndan, Erin C., Rhel, Kieran, Rafael P, Sarah, and Melanie B. Little did they know that by supporting one little Kickstarter, they'd find a permanent spot on my acknowledgments page.

ABOUT THE AUTHOR

Jules Crisare loves writing sexy shifter romances. The growly and dominant males of Broken Peak and the Silver Sentinels are the ones bending to the strong wills of the smart heroines who cross their paths. Seriously, only strong heroines need apply to capture the hearts of these sexy alphas. Get your shifter loving fingers ready to turn those pages and explore the world of the Sentinels of the Silver Orb.

www.JCrisare.com